Cathy Carne had also been told something in her damned letter.

But there were other provisions of the will, dismissed as harmless jokes, but were they? A tube of Winsor blue for Alan Tate, spectacles for Burger . . . 'which I hope may improve his judgement and help him to see the obvious.' To see the obvious – Wycliffe wished that spectacles might do that for him. What was obvious? The relative merits of Tate's and Edwin's paintings? That was Burger's explanation but the truth might not be so innocent.

A tube of Winsor blue for Alan Tate – a way of wishing him luck, Cathy Carne had said.

Wycliffe resigned himself to lying awake for the rest of the night but, in fact, he fell asleep and knew nothing more until he was awakened to broad daylight and seagulls squawking outside his window.

W.J. Burley lived near Newquay in Cornwall, and was a schoolmaster until he retired to concentrate on his writing. His many Wycliffe books include, most recently, *Wycliffe and the Guild of Nine*. He died in 2002.

By W.J. Burley

Wycliffe
AND THE
WINSOR BLUE

W.J.Burley

An Orion paperback

First published in Great Britain in 1987
by Victor Gollancz Ltd
First published in paperback in 1989
by Corgi Books
This paperback edition published in 2004
by Orion Books Ltd,
Orion House, 5 Upper St Martin's Lane,
London WC2H 9EA

3 5 7 8 6 4 2

A CIP catalogue record for this book
is available from the British Library.

ISBN-13 978-0-7528-5873-9
ISBN-10 0-7528-5873-4

Printed and bound in Great Britain by
Clays Ltd, St Ives plc

The Orion Publishing Group's policy is to use papers that
are natural, renewable and recyclable products and
made from wood grown in sustainable forests. The logging
and manufacturing processes are expected to conform to
the environmental regulations of the country of origin.

www.orionbooks.co.uk

To my wife:
critic and collaborator

People who know the town of Falmouth may be irritated by inaccuracies in the topography. These are deliberate in order to avoid any risk that a real person might be identified with one of the characters in this book – all of whom are imaginary.

W.J.B.

CHAPTER ONE

Edwin Garland felt uneasy, a vague shapeless unease for which he could find no immediate cause.

'You haven't taken any ham, father.'

'What?'

Beryl lifted a slice of ham on to his plate. 'Are you feeling all right, father?'

'Of course I'm feeling all right! Why shouldn't I?' In fact, he was feeling quite queer.

His son, Francis, was munching away, his protuberant eyes fixed on his father in an unwavering stare.

Beryl was beginning to look like an old woman; her hair was lank and grey, and there were fine wrinkles about her mouth . . . And that nose which seemed to sharpen with the years made her look predatory . . . How old was she? Fifty-five? About that . . . Nine years older than Francis . . . That gap . . . Why was she always so damned miserable? Of course she was drinking on the sly, her and her precious friend . . .

He was really feeling strange, curiously detached, but he struggled to hold on. His thoughts seemed to wander out of control . . . They were watching him. Concentrate on something! He looked at his wife's portrait which hung on the wall opposite where he sat. Gifford Tate had painted it a few weeks before she died. A fair painting; free in style but at the same time a good likeness. Gifford had gone overboard a bit in the blues though . . . For some reason this thought made Edwin chuckle to himself.

Francis's owl-like countenance obtruded again. Francis was too fat, his face was podgy and he had a paunch. Soft! Too much food, too little exercise. Greedy from childhood . . . Hard to credit that he had once fathered a daughter – and a beautiful girl she had turned out to be – like her granny . . . Funny thing, heredity; hit and miss. Anna was twenty now, living with her mother and some randy young rooster who knew when he was well off.

His thoughts returned to his wife's portrait. The Dresden China look. 'Refinement and fragility' Gifford had said. He was right: Judith had been . . . Judith had been exquisite – that was the word. And a bitch, but that was another story.

What was the matter with him? He was confused; and that was another word, an unpleasant one in the ears of a man of seventy-five. Mealy mouthed jargon for senile. Better eat some of this bloody ham or they would think . . . He pushed it around with his fork. Soggy! How did they make the stuff hold all that water? An offence to water milk so why not ham?

Back to Beryl and Francis. What a pair! They were Judith's children, so why were they so damned unprepossessing? And they had mean, scheming little minds. He had supported them all their lives and what had they ever done for him except wait for him to die? Watching, like vultures . . . Well, they wouldn't have long to wait, now, but they had a surprise or two to come.

He caught sight of Beryl's head in profile. Her mother's daughter, but Beryl *exquisite*! He wanted to laugh. What the hell was wrong with him? Time to pull himself together.

Safer to look out of the window, concentrate on the

view; that had never let him down. The living-room was at the back of the house, overlooking the harbour, and from where he sat at table he could see right across Carrick Roads to St Just-in-Roseland. Sunlight glittered on the water and the colours . . . the colours were not bright, but the light shattered in reflection, was brilliant. How often had he struggled to make that distinction on canvas? Painting light: that was what it was all about. The Impressionists had tried, God knows! but even they . . .

'I think I shall go down to the studio.'

Beryl said: 'But you've eaten hardly anything, father! Really —'

'I've had enough.' And he added under his breath: 'More than enough!' without being quite sure what he meant.

'Shall I bring your coffee down to you?'

'No.'

'You haven't had your tablets . . .'

'For Christ's sake!'

He went down the stairs, holding tight to the bannisters and swaying slightly. He felt giddy.

He had been born and lived all his life over the shop: E. Garland and Son, Artists' Suppliers and Printers. In the little hall at the bottom of the stairs one door opened into a side passage leading to the street; the other, to the back of the shop through which he had to pass to reach the studio. The shop was closed for the lunch hour. He shuffled past well ordered, dusted shelves and racks, and past the little office where his father had sat and schemed for most of his life. The place was peopled with ghosts and soon he would be one of them. He fumbled with a key from his pocket then opened a door into another world.

Like the living-room upstairs his studio looked out

9

on the harbour. It was more like a workshop than a studio – a painter's workshop. There was a sturdy bench, with an orderly arrangement of tools, where he made stretchers and frames. There was an earthenware sink, a table, a couple of easels, a painter's trolley, a chest of shallow drawers. Empty frames and canvases were stacked against the walls . . . And almost every object in the room seemed to be spattered with multi-coloured splashes of paint; while the windows were covered with grime and festooned with cob-webs. A scruffy orderliness. That was how he liked it.

When Gifford Tate was alive and used to visit him, Tate had croaked through his beard: 'Why the hell don't you get yourself a decent studio, Eddie? God knows you can afford it! At least get somebody to clean the bloody windows!' And Garland had answered: 'I like it as it is, and as for the windows, that muck is a natural filter for the light and if any interfering bastard ever cleaned 'em I'd twist his credentials off.'

Entering his studio always gave his spirit a lift; it did so now.

He fetched a tobacco pouch out of his pocket and a packet of cigarette papers. With a lifetime of practice behind him he rolled a passable cigarette in his fingers and lit it.

There was a painting on one of the easels and the trolley with his brushes, tubes of paint, and palette was beside it. He pulled up a high stool and stood, his bottom propped on the stool, which he used like a shooting stick, his painting posture for these latter days. The painting seemed complete: another harbour scene. He studied it with growing distaste. 'That water . . . as exciting as a sludge pit in a sewage works.'

He closed his eyes and tried with all the concentration of which he was capable to see with his mind exactly what it was that he had wanted to paint. Slowly the scene seemed to materialise once more out of his imagination: the mist, the swathe of sunlit water; the water like shot silk in the shelter of the boats; ripples elsewhere, tiny vibrant glittering crests . . . Points of pure light . . . so brilliant that they hurt the eyes . . .

God! How they hurt the eyes! But for once he believed that he was seeing as he had striven all his life to see . . . Diamond points . . . blinding! They seemed to sear into his brain. He groped vaguely with his right hand as though reaching for a brush and as he did so he experienced an intolerable contraction in his chest, a paralysing pain, and with a cry of anguish he fell, taking the stool with him.

His niece, Cathy Carne, found him when she came back to open the shop after lunch. She was surprised to see the studio door open, he always closed the door when he was working and kept it locked when he wasn't there. Then she saw him, his heavy body lying mounded over the stool which had fallen with him. His jaw sagged and his eyes stared.

Her first reaction was incredulity. The old man had been with her in the shop that morning, the same as ever, gossiping about the business, about the vagaries of their customers, the oddities of town councillors and the perverseness of families – all with a humour that was wickedly spiced. Of course he had been warned; the family had been warned, but . . .

She felt empty inside.

She went upstairs. On the landing she could hear voices coming from the living-room and she pushed open the door. Beryl was clearing the table; Francis, with his hands in his pockets, was staring out of the window. There was an atmosphere, as always when the two of them were left alone together.

11

Beryl looked at her: 'What's wrong?'

'It's uncle; he's collapsed in the studio.' She added after a pause: 'He's dead.'

Without a word Francis turned away fom the window and pushed past her. They heard his heavy footsteps descending the stairs.

Cathy picked up the telephone which stood on a side table. 'I'd better telephone Alan.'

She dialled a number and spoke to the receptionist. 'I'm speaking for Mr Garland at the art shop. Is Dr Tate there?' A pause and when she spoke again her manner was familiar: 'Oh, Alan – Cathy here. I'm afraid it's bad news . . . Yes, Uncle . . . he collapsed on the floor in the studio . . . I'm afraid so . . . If you will . . . Yes, come to the side door.'

She replaced the receiver and turned to Beryl. 'He'll be here in a few minutes.'

Beryl was standing motionless in the middle of the room, her hand on her heart. 'I knew something was going to happen; I could *feel* it! And he brought it on himself.'

Cathy said: 'We'd better go down.'

They went downstairs; Francis was standing in the doorway of the studio. 'Well, he's dead all right.'

'I telephoned the surgery.'

'Good!'

Cathy was looking past him into the studio. 'Can't we move him?'

'Better not.'

Beryl said: 'I've told him and told him but he took no notice . . . He wouldn't even take the tablets Alan gave him. He brought it on himself.'

And then it occurred to Cathy that although the old man was lying exactly as she had seen him, something had changed. Surely, there was a different picture on the easel? Odd! She was on the point of saying something but changed her mind. After all, what difference could it make? If Francis was up to something it was nothing to do with her.

Francis, hands thrust deep into his trouser pockets, said: 'I thought he seemed a bit queer at lunch but I didn't expect it to come to this . . .'

They stood, silent and waiting, until the side door opened and Alan Tate came in. He was slight of build, very dark, with a sallow complexion, and meticulously dressed in a dark grey suit with a silk tie. Son of Gifford Tate, the painter, he had been the Garlands' doctor since, at his father's death, he had returned to Falmouth and set up practice in the family house.

Subdued greetings, then he went about his business. A brief examination, his movements rapid and sure. He spoke in staccato phrases: 'His heart gave out, that's what it amounts to. Bound to happen sooner or later . . . Give me a hand, Francis – get the stool out from under him; straighten him up a little.' Although first names were being used his attitude and manner were strictly professional.

Beryl said: 'We can't leave him here, he'll have to be taken upstairs.'

Tate looked up at her, his brown eyes enlarged by the lenses of his spectacles. 'He's a big man, Beryl; too much for Francis and me. The undertakers will do it and it will be more decent that way.'

Francis said: 'You'll come upstairs, Alan?'

Tate glanced at his watch. 'I can spare a few minutes.'

Cathy Carne said: 'Shouldn't we tell Uncle Thomas and Mark?'

Blank looks from Beryl and Francis.

'After all, Thomas is his brother.'

Beryl said: 'They'll hear soon enough.'

Cathy gave up. 'Do you want me to shut the shop?'

'The shop?' Francis turned his bulging eyes on her: 'What would be the point of that?'

Cathy stayed in the shop while the others went upstairs. Ten minutes later Tate came down alone. Cathy was in the little office and he came to stand in the doorway. 'They are both quite composed. I doubt if there will be any problem with delayed shock.' Cynical. 'You found him, I gather?'

'Yes.'

'A shock for you. They've been in touch with the undertaker and when I left they were arguing about the funeral.'

'When shall I see you again?'

Tate hesitated. 'I'll telephone.' And added, seemingly in explanation: 'Marcella is very depressed. I'm concerned about her.'

Cathy was feeling the heat; little beads of perspiration formed between her shoulder blades and breasts. She had worn a full-length coat because it was all she had that was decently subfusc; now she wished that she had been less conformist.

She was staring at the coffin, the wooden box with fancy trimmings which held the mortal remains of Edwin Garland, her uncle and employer. She wondered what his comment would have been had he been in a position to make one.

'Man that is born of woman hath but a short time to live and is full of misery . . .'

They weren't talking about Edwin Garland; Edwin had enjoyed life in his own way.

There were more wreaths than she would have expected and the flowers were already wilting in the merciless sun. She wondered who had sent them all.

Francis, as chief mourner, stood next to the vicar; his paunchiness exaggerated by an old, dark suit that was too small for him. She wondered about the bruise on his cheek: she had noticed it the evening before when he came back from his Tuesday round. 'I walked into a door.' Somebody had hit him. Interesting!

With glazed eyes he was staring into the middle distance. Day-dreaming of life after the shop? More than likely. It wouldn't be long before he closed a deal with one or other of the chain stores who had shown an interest in the site. Then there was the printing works . . . Francis had never shown any real interest in either side of the business and, as far as the shop was concerned, this had meant that Cathy had been free to go her own way under the old man's eye.

Beryl would have to move out, but she would go to live with her friend; two old-maids together. It was what they both wanted and with her share of her father's money Beryl would be well able to provide for both of them in style.

'And that leaves me . . . At thirty-six.'

She had had a letter from Edwin's solicitor asking her to come to his office the following day. It must mean that she had been mentioned in the will. A picture, probably; she had always admired his work, perhaps a little money to go with it; that would be welcome.

' . . . deliver us not into the bitter pains of eternal death.'

Yes, well, it might not be as bad as that.

It was Wednesday afternoon. In the tradition of the street Edwin was being buried on early closing day so that the other traders could attend. But the custom had lost its meaning because there were so few private traders left, and company managers are faceless men, here today and gone tomorrow. All the same, there was a good crowd, the more surprising because Francis had not bothered to organise anything properly.

It was one of the hottest days of the year and the new part of the cemetery was without trees.. Most people were out enjoying themselves and she could hear children on the beach which was not far away.

Francis's illegitimate daughter, Anna, was there with her boyfriend. They stood a little way back from the others as though unsure of their right to be there at all, and they were in bizarre contrast to the rest of the mourners. The girl's fair hair was scraped back and held with a slide; she wore a grey shirt, open half-way down the front, and bleached jeans. Her boyfriend had his hair down to his shoulders and wore a bandeau. His sweat-shirt carried the slogan: 'No! to Trident!', and his jeans seemed about to fall apart. Both of them were so beautifully and evenly brown that clothes seemed superfluous.

Cathy looked at them with a mixture of envy and doubt. At their age she had already spent four years working in her uncle's shop. But what would they be doing at thirty-six?

Also standing well back from the grave, Mike Treloar, the printing works foreman, supported himself on a stick. As a boy he had been crippled by polio.

Cathy was almost opposite Alan Tate and he was watching her, or seemed to be. It was hard to tell because of the sun glinting on his glasses. Looked at objectively there was nothing special about him: a smallish man, slight of build, dark-brown hair *en brosse*, spectacles with thick lenses and a broad, carefully trimmed moustache. Everything about him was meticulous, as though the parts had been made and assembled with scrupulous care. Cathy sometimes wondered why women found him so attractive, why she herself did.

He was with Marcella, his father's second wife and widow. In her late thirties, she was two or three years younger than her step-son. Once she had been attractive, with a good figure: now she was painfully thin and her sharp features gave her a pinched look. She did nothing to improve her appearance; her flaxen hair was cut short so that it fitted her head like a helmet and accentuated the angularity of her features.

Cathy was surprised how ill she looked, there was an area of paleness about her eyes, and her nose was pinched and reddened about the nostrils; perhaps a summer cold, though Alan had said she was depressed.

'Forasmuch as it hath pleased Almighty God of his great mercy . . .'

When the service was over there was the ritual of shaking hands with the vicar. Francis spoke with his daughter and the boy. Beryl chatted with one or two of the bystanders then lingered to look at the cards on the wreaths and this annoyed Francis.

'Come *on*, Beryl! The undertaker will give you a list.'

Franics had not hired cars and Cathy joined him and Beryl in his ten-year-old saloon. As they drove away from the cemetery she spotted the clapped-out van belonging to Anna's boyfriend parked some distance from the gates, a large CND symbol painted on its side.

Beryl sat in the back of the car, her large black handbag with brass fittings balanced on her knees. She delved into the bag and came up with a packet of pastilles which she began to suck, filling the car with a sickly sweet smell.

She said: 'The Tates were there and they sent a big wreath; we ought to have invited them back with us.'

Francis did not answer.

17

Beryl went on: 'I saw you talking to Anna and that boy. Very friendly all of a sudden.' It was an accusation.

'Why not? She's my daughter, isn't she?'

Conversation between brother and sister was conducted at a level of mutual aggression which stopped just short of exploding into a row. An exercise in brinkmanship.

'What did she say?'

'Not a lot.'

'Did she ask where you got your bruises from?'

At first it seemed that Francis was going to leave it at that, the ball in his court, but in fact he was trying to decide which would annoy her most: being kept in the dark about his conversation with Anna or knowing the truth. He decided to speak: 'She said she'd had a letter from the lawyer.'

Beryl was roused. 'Why should Shrimpton write to her?'

'I suppose father has left her something; he had a soft spot for Anna, he said she looked like mother.'

Beryl made an angry movement. 'I only hope he's had more sense than to leave her money! She may look like mother, but mother would have turned in her grave if she could have seen that girl today!'

Cathy said: 'I had a letter from Shrimpton, myself. It simply asked me to come to his office tomorrow afternoon at half-past two.'

Beryl was dismissive. 'Yes, dear, that was to be expected. He was bound to remember you with a little legacy. This is quite different! Quite different!'

To further annoy his sister, Francis said: 'Anna is his granddaughter after all.' But the exchange had sown a tiny seed of doubt in his own mind . . .

Francis parked the car and they walked along the

18

street to the shop. When they were in the little hall at the foot of the stairs Francis said: 'Is father's studio locked, Cathy?'

'I don't think so, but the key is in the door.'

'Then lock it and bring the key up with you.'

Beryl said: 'What's this about?'

He turned his sullen gaze on her but did not answer.

Upstairs, Beryl's friend had made coffee and sandwiches for them.

Francis stood by the window. 'There's a mist coming in.'

Beryl's friend said: 'Yes, but they said on the radio that it would be fine again tomorrow.'

Francis sat at his desk making entries on index cards. He wrote in a small, neat, but cramped hand, pausing now and then to refer to one or other of the books and papers spread on his desk. On a two-deck trolley to his right a V.D.U. stood above a computer keyboard. The screen displayed columns of figures against groups of code letters and from time to time Francis referred to these, scrolling the display on or back.

The room in which he worked had been his bedroom since infancy, though now the only evidence of its primary purpose was a narrow divan bed. One wall was wholly taken up with books while the other walls were hung with home-produced charts in which numbers and symbols formed elaborate geometrical patterns. There was a bank of card-index drawers and a multi-drawer filing cabinet.

Francis seemed wholly absorbed, yet once or twice he sat back in his chair and told himself: 'My father is dead!' It was as though he could not be convinced; as though he could hardly accept the fact that his father was no longer there, the final arbiter of all that happened in the business and in their domestic lives. He was like a goldfish, suddenly tipped out of its bowl into a pond, conditioned to continue swimming in circles. Yet his father's death should not have come as a surprise. Six months ago Alan Tate had said: 'His heart is by no means strong and his blood pressure being what it is . . . If only he would discipline himself to regular medication and give up smoking . . .' Of course Francis had thought about it as something that was inevitable, and he had plans, but they had never seemed very real and he had looked on them as castles in the air. Now . . .

His desk was placed near the window, overlooking the narrow canyon of the street. At this time of night the street was quiet: the occasional car, and now and then a group of rowdy youths asserting their masculinity like stags in rut. Although it was dark outside he had not drawn the curtains. Silvery streaks of rain appeared out of the darkness and trickled down the shining panes. A wall clock ticked loudly: a few minutes to nine. Mitch, his black and white terrier, was asleep in a wicker basket on the floor. Beryl and her friend were in the living-room, across the passage.

At a quarter past nine there was a tap at the door; Beryl came in and stood waiting for his attention. She wore a long raincoat which drooped from her thin shoulders and she carried a small overnight bag. Her pale face was blotched and her lips were moist. When he turned towards her she said: 'I'm not staying in the house tonight, Francis, I'm too upset. I'm going back with Celia but I shall be here in time to get your breakfast in the morning.'

He merely stared at her with his bulging eyes and she went on: 'There are biscuits in the tin by the cooker and there is plenty of milk if you want to make yourself a hot drink.'

In a flat voice, the more insulting by its indifference, he said: 'You don't have to bother about me. Move in with Celia whenever you want.' And he turned back to his desk.

She would have liked to make some cutting rejoinder but none came to mind so she went out, closing the door behind her.

At ten o'clock he switched off his computer and put away his books. Mitch skipped out of his basket, tail wagging, and they went downstairs together. In the little hall, Francis put on a waterproof coat and cap and they went out by the back door.

The shops on the Garlands' side of the street backed on the water and only a narrow paved walk separated them from the harbour. At ten o'clock each evening, except in the very worst weather, Francis and his dog took their walk along the waterfront as far as the yacht marina and returned by the street.

It was dark for an August night. The lights at the docks twinkled mistily, and some of the larger craft at moorings carried lights, but for the most part the harbour was a broad plain of darkness. It was of no consequence; Garland knew every step of the way and Mitch trotted ahead, pursuing an erratic course as he nosed out the rich odours brought to him on the moist air.

For Francis this nightly constitutional had its place in a larger fantasy. He liked to imagine himself an academic, working after dinner in one of those elegant book-lined rooms of an Oxford college. As the clocks chimed and struck all over the city he would stroll down the Broad, along St Giles and round by the Parks . . . Nature, he thought, had intended him for scholarship yet here he was at forty-six, still a small-town tradesman.

21

Well that at any rate would change.

'My father is dead!' Well, he couldn't be expected to shed any tears.

There had been offers for the shop which his father had consistently turned down. Offers for the site, not the business. One, a very good one from a firm of chain-store chemists, was still open. In a few months he could leave those rooms over the shop and the shop itself for ever. Of course Cathy Carne was being difficult, already there had been an outburst over something he had said. The old man had spoiled her and it was high time that she faced facts.

Then there was the printing works: it had kept pace with the changing times and if it was put on the market there would be plenty of interest. Then he would be free! As far back as he could remember, those phrases 'the shop' and 'the works' had been spoken by his parents with a certain solemnity, as some speak of 'the church' or 'the monarchy'. Well, all that was over.

Their walk along the wharf was interrupted by a car-park where a scatttering of vehicles gleamed in the jaundiced light of a sodium lamp. To his surprise he recognised the battered old van which belonged to Anna's boyfriend and he wondered what it was doing there. Then he saw the glowing tip of someone's cigarette behind the windshield. He continued his walk and thought no more about the van.

'My father is dead!'

In a year the shop would be no more, lorries would carry away the rubble to which it had been reduced, leaving a gap to be filled by yet another chain store. Would he then feel a certain sadness? He thought not: at this moment the prospect afforded him a satisfaction that was almost spiteful in its intensity.

Sentiment and nostalgia are for pleasant memories.

A white yacht carrying navigation lights glided in ghostly silence through the seeming maze of moored craft, putting out to sea. He stopped to watch her until she disappeared in the darkness. The tide was lapping the harbour wall within a yard of his feet.

He would have enough money to live comfortably and he would never be bored. For many years his studies had absorbed every moment of his spare time, now they would be his full-time occupation. He would be able to visit libraries, museums and institutions all over Britain and make contact with other numerologists. Even abroad . . . He was resolved to meet every possible criticism in advance and, eventually, his conclusions would be presented to the world in a scholarly book.

And if in this new life he was to be alone . . . well, he had been alone for most of his life. In his twenties he had taken up with a girl called Freda and got her pregnant. She had given birth to a daughter but Freda had been no more anxious to marry than he had. Since then she had married someone else and been widowed, but she still lived in the district with their daughter, Anna. He saw Anna occasionally but he had not seen Freda for years though he had to admit that he might not have recognised her had he passed her in the street.

Recently he had formed another attachment, one which he valued more. But there was a price to be paid in this relationship and he wasn't sure . . . He couldn't stand scenes; violence of any sort appalled him . . .

Involuntarily he raised his hand to his face.

They were approaching a point where the wharf walk was bridged over by scaffolding erected to repair the back wall of Benson's furniture shop. Warning lights on the steel supports blinked feebly through the mist.

Mitch growled, then yelped.

'Quiet, boy!'

He had no sense of foreboding, no intimation of danger; on the contrary he felt light hearted, even light headed as vistas of freedom seemed to open ahead of him. Mitch scampered under the scaffolding and Garland followed. The lowest tier of planks cleared his head by at least a foot.

As he emerged at the other end he was aware of a frightful, blinding, stunning pain in his head, and then nothing.

CHAPTER TWO

Chief Superintendent Wycliffe's driver pulled into the car park, which had been closed to the public, and joined a line of police vehicles. A uniformed man, there to ward off sightseers, saluted.

On his way down to take part in an official inspection, Wycliffe had monitored reports on his car radio and so arrived at the scene of crime before his headquarters had got a team together. The Deputy Chief Constable, in his parade uniform, would have to manage the inspection without the assistance of his head of C.I.D.

Falmouth: a town he liked. J.B. Priestley once said that it could never quite make up its mind whether it was a port or a resort, but that very ambivalence had saved it from the worst pitfalls of both. The harbour looked mysterious: the sun had broken through but mist still lay over the docks. Massive superstructures; squat, tapering funnels; slender masts, and the jibs of cranes, merged in a ghostly silhouette. Elsewhere in the harbour the moored yachts, the power boats, launches and dinghies, regimented by the tide, matched colourful reflections in the water.

Wycliffe was reminded of a busman's holiday he had spent, not so long ago, across at St Mawes.

Appraised by bush telegraph or E.S.P. of his advent, Divisional Chief Inspector Reed hurried along the wharf to greet him.

'A nasty business, sir. Very nasty!'

A shaking of hands and a brief excursion into reminiscence. 'This way . . . He's just beyond that scaffolding . . . The surgeon has been and gone, he reckons death probably took place early in the night; the coroner has been informed, and the scenes-of-crime chaps are on the job . . .'

They walked together along the wharf; the two men, in striking contrast. Reed was built on an over-generous scale, bull-necked and bulging in his grey pinstripe; Wycliffe, slight of build, and rather pale, was more likely to be taken for an academic than a policeman; hard to believe that he had served a tough apprenticeship on the beat in a Midland city.

The scenes-of-crime van was parked as near the site as it could get, planks had been laid on the ground approaching and under the scaffolding to preserve whatever evidence there might be, and the area where the body was had been screened off. The scenes-of-crime officers had photographed the dead man and the ground for some distance around. Footprints, found in soft mud under the scaffolding, had been photographed and casts made though there was little doubt that they belonged to the victim, not the killer. There were dog prints too. The whole area was littered with fragments of mortar which had been chipped out of the wall by workmen getting it ready for re-pointing.

Behind the screen Wycliffe looked down at the dead man: middle or late forties, probably above average height, bony, but with a tendency to corpulence – sedentary: the disease of modern man. He wore a fawn waterproof, cord trousers, and good quality brown shoes. The left side of his face, in the region of the jaw articulation, looked at first sight as though it had been smashed by a blow, but Wycliffe recognised it as the

wound of exit of a bullet which had probably ricochet-
ted inside the skull. Bending down, he looked for and
found the wound of entry, a small round hole in the top
of the head towards the back. The thin, fair hair had
been singed and stained around the wound.

The undamaged part of the face had a puffy softness,
an appearance of immaturity, accentuated by a fair
moustache of wispy growth. There was an area of
bruising below the right eye but, although it was recent,
Wycliffe felt sure that it had been inflicted some time
before death – probably the day before.

Reed, standing behind him, said: 'A fight?'

'Perhaps, at least several hours before he was killed.'

Murder, that much was evident but the motive was
not. They had found the man's wallet in the pocket of
his jacket with forty pounds in notes, a credit card, and
a driving licence in the name of Francis Garland.

Wycliffe brooded. In the ensuing hours and days he
would get to know Francis Garland perhaps better than
he knew many of his colleagues and acquaintances. His
data would come from relatives and friends, from those
not so friendly; from the man's habits, likes and
dislikes, his loves and his hates. In the end, if this crime
turned out to be something more than an abortive
mugging, he would have a portrait of the victim and
through that portrait some indication of why he had
become one.

Reed volunteered background: 'The Garlands have a
shop in the main street, a couple of hundred yards from
here: artists' materials, pictures, that sort of thing;
they're printers too – they have their works farther
along the waterfront, just beyond Customs Quay. You
can see it from here – that concrete building. Anyway,
this chap lived with his father and sister in the rooms
over the shop – until Saturday.'

'What happened on Saturday?'

'His father died of a stroke. A bit of a coincidence, don't you think?'

'Has anyone broken the news to the sister?'

'I've sent Pritchard; he's good on bereavements. Ought to have been an undertaker.'

'So Garland was unmarried?'

'Yes, but according to the local sergeant, there's an illegitimate daughter around somewhere.'

The first bits of the jig-saw. From now on he would be looking for some sort of pattern. He would spend a great deal of time trying to fit in fresh pieces only to find that most of them didn't belong to his picture. Criminal investigation is a sad story of false trails and dead ends.

'Was he a queer?'

'Not as far as we know, but it's possible.'

The church clock doled out ten strokes on its tinny bell. Looking down at the dead man Wycliffe felt guilty because he was experiencing a sense of mild elation. He loathed the sterile ritual of inspections, and this poor devil in his untimely end had saved him from that. He slipped easily into the routine of a murder inquiry.

'Garland's sister must have realised that her brother didn't come home last night.'

'You would think so.'

'Who found him?'

'The builder's men coming to work on this wall. They had the sense not to plough in and now they're laying off until they hear from us.' Reed removed his fisherman's hat, uncovering a bald crown and a fringe of auburn hair. With a large pocket handkerchief he wiped the perspiration from his forehead; it was getting hot.

There was blood on the ground from the exit wound

which had not been entirely washed away by the overnight rain. The man must have been shot from above at close range as he emerged from under the scaffolding. Wycliffe looked up at the first tier of planks; the shot must have been fired from up there. If the attack went wrong the assailant stood a good chance of not being identified and if it was apparently successful it would be safe to come down and make sure.

He called to Fox, the sergeant in charge of scene of crime. Fox looked like Bertie Wooster and, for some reason, was known as Brenda to his colleagues. He was good at his job, though not as good as he thought he was, and his smugness irritated Wycliffe.

'Take a look up there where the killer must have stood or knelt.'

Fox assumed a judicial air. 'I thought it better to concentrate on the ground —'

'Just do as I ask, Fox. Now, please.'

There was no point in staying at the scene. Fox and the others would do all that was necessary and a good deal that wasn't, working by the book.

He reassured Reed about local assistance. 'I know you must have a full load so I'll try not to be greedy. I'm going to talk to somebody at the shop – the sister if possible.'

He walked back along the wharf to the car park. On an R.T. link from his car he spoke to his deputy, John Scales, at headquarters. 'Who've you got for me, John?'

The composition of a team depends on who happens to be doing what at the time. Apart from Detective Inspector Kersey, Wycliffe's usual number one, Scales had sent Sergeants Shaw and Lane. Shaw was a good organiser and internal collator, well versed in computer mystique. Lucy Lane enjoyed the distinction of having convinced Wycliffe that a woman could more than hold her own in the serious crimes squad and not only in rape cases. The three of them, with four detective constables, would set the ball rolling.

Wycliffe left his car on the park and climbed the slope to the street.

Falmouth's main shopping street runs narrowly and crookedly along the waterfront with shops on both sides but with occasional tantalising glimpses of the harbour. The street is in three parts: Market Street, because there was once a market; Church Street, because of the Church of King Charles the Martyr, built at the Restoration; and Arwenack Street, because it leads eventually to Arwenack House, all that is left of the home of the Killigrews, a mixed bag of soldiers, dramatists, pirates and entrepreneurs, who founded the town and built the church.

As is usual until mid-morning, the street was jammed with vans and lorries unloading, taking up pavement as well as road, so that shoppers had to plot a course through a maze of obstacles. Tourists navigated with resigned expressions: this was Holiday and at least you could understand the lingo.

It was sixteen years since Wycliffe's last case in the town and he was recapturing the atmosphere of the place. For centuries merchant seamen from all over the world have mingled with the local population and now, in addition, for three months every year, holiday-makers flood in like the tide. Yet the substratum of true locals remains, a distinct, identifiable breed, preserving the town's unique parochialism and delighting in the frustration of imported bureaucrats.

Byron, who had no good word to say of the town itself, spoke highly of its inhabitants: '. . . both female and male, at least the young ones, are remarkably handsome, and how the devil they came to be so is a wonder.'

'E. Garland and Son: Artists' Suppliers and Printers': gilt letters on a green ground; a discreet double frontage between a supermarket and a bank. One window displayed easels, folding stools, palettes, stretched canvases, and various shoulder-bags for transporting all the impedimenta of the would-be *plein air* painter; in the other window there were paintings of varied merit and price. There was a framed notice which read: 'Orders taken for printing of all kinds, commercial and private. Estimates on request without obligation.'

Wycliffe decided to avoid the shop for the moment; the family lived in the rooms above so there was probably a separate entrance. He found it in a stone-flagged side passage, a door bearing a small brass plate: 'Garland'. He rang the bell and it was answered by a youngish woman wearing a blue overall.

'Miss Garland?'

'No, what do you want?'

Wycliffe would have been surprised if she had said yes.

He introduced himself and she responded with engaging candour: 'Cathy Carne – I work in the shop. A policeman came earlier to break the news to Miss Garland.'

The woman was slim, dark, and well made, with an air of reserve that made one take her seriously. Dark blue eyes and black lashes: a felicitous dip from the genetic bran tub.

'It must have been a shock to Miss Garland, coming so soon after her father's death.'

'It was. I suppose you want to speak to her? She has a friend with her just now.'

On the spur of the moment he said: 'I would like to talk to you first.'

'If you wish.'

A door from the hall opened into the back of the shop. 'Through here.' She took him into a small office with a window overlooking the harbour. Desk, typewriter, telephone, safe, filing cabinet – all very modern and giving an impression of crisp business-like efficiency.

'Do sit down.'

She picked up a cigarette pack from the desk. 'Smoke? . . . No? Do you mind if I do?' She lit a cigarette and inhaled with sensual enjoyment.

'Do you mind telling me your position here, Miss Carne?' She was clearly more than a shop assistant.

A ghost of a smile. 'I sometimes wonder. I suppose you could say that I'm a kind of manageress. Anyway I've been here twenty years – since I left school, and Edwin Garland was my uncle by marriage.'

'Do you live above the shop?'

'I do not!' Emphatic.

'When you arrived this morning did you see Miss Garland at once?'

'She was waiting for me. She said it looked as though Francis hadn't been home all night and she was worried.'

'Had she been worried all night?'

'She wasn't here. She spent the night at a friend's house – the one who is with her now. When she returned home this morning she found Francis's dog, Mitch, whimpering outside the back door. Francis always takes him for a walk last thing before going to bed. It was while we were deciding what to do that your policeman turned up with the news.'

She was calm, self-possessed, incisive, and not obviously distressed.

A young girl, also wearing a blue overall, came into the office. After a brief apology she said: 'Is it all right to allow credit for this, Miss Carne?' She held out a bill form.

'Yes, that will be all right, Alice, but get Mrs Wilson to sign the bill and make sure the signature comes through on the carbon.'

Wycliffe said: 'Could anyone who knew your cousin's habits rely on him taking the same walk at approximately the same time each night?'

'Short of an earthquake or a deluge.'

'Do you know of any reason why he might have been killed?'

She shook her head. 'No. Francis wasn't the sort to make friends and influence people but I can't believe that anybody would want to murder him.'

'Somebody already has,' Wycliffe said. 'I'm told that there is a daughter?'

'It didn't take you long to find that out. Anna is twenty.'

'She lives with her mother?'

'And her boyfriend. By the way, somebody should tell her. After all he was her father.'

'Did he keep in touch with her?'

She trickled out a spiral of smoke and watched it rise. 'She kept in touch with him – at intervals.'

'Filial affection?'

She laughed outright. 'I'm in no position to say. My guess would be an upsurge of sentiment whenever the money was getting tight. But then, I'm a cynic.'

'They live near here?'

'In Flushing, just across the water. Shortly after Anna was born her mother married, and a year or so ago her husband died leaving her the house and a little money. The boyfriend moved in at the beginning of the

33

summer; he gets by doing casual work on the farms.'
She was watching him through the cigarette smoke to
judge the effect she was producing.

A capable woman, nobody's fool; but was she
adopting a deliberate pose? And if so, for what
purpose?

'Does Anna have a job?'

'She's on the check-out in one of the supermarkets
but I think she's on holiday this week.'

'Any other relatives?'

She smiled. 'Yes, but not acknowledged. Edwin's
younger brother Thomas and his son, Mark. Mark is
about my age and also unmarried.'

'Local?'

'Oh, yes. The two of them live in a house near the
docks. Thomas is a retired schoolteacher and Mark is a
chiropractor – some sort of osteopath.'

'You said they weren't acknowledged; what's wrong
with them from the Edwin Garlands' point of view?'

'Thirty years ago Thomas contested his father's will,
he lost but his action split the family; I don't think
there's been any contact since.'

'Thomas didn't go to his brother's funeral?'

'No, but I saw Mark lurking in the background as
though he didn't want to be seen. He's an odd fish.'

Wycliffe changed the subject. 'You don't seem very
distressed by your cousin's death.'

She considered this. 'I suppose not. Of course I'm
very sorry but our relationship has never been close. I
worked for his father – my uncle, not for Francis.'

'But surely Francis was involved?'

She tapped ash from her cigarette. 'With the printing
and outside sales. Two days a week – Mondays and
Tuesdays – he went out with the van delivering orders
to customers and taking new ones for both the printing

and the art sides. The rest of the week he was at the printing works. He didn't interfere here, Uncle saw to that, so I've had a free hand in the shop and although I say it myself I've made a go of it.'

She made an irritable movement. 'There's no point in mincing words. Francis has never been interested in the business and he's never pulled his weight. Although he was supposed to be in charge of the printing works it was the foreman, Mike Treloar, who ran it with Uncle keeping an eye on things and deciding policy. Francis's one idea, if he'd lived, would have been to sell out. The printing works is a good investment for anybody's money and this site is a key one in the street. Uncle had several offers but he turned them all down.'

'When we found Francis his face was marked by fairly recent bruising. Do you know how and when it happened?'

'No, I saw the bruise when he came back to the shop on Tuesday evening and I asked him what he'd done to himself. He just growled something about having walked into a door.'

Wycliffe was trying to make up his mind about Cathy Carne. A good business woman, intelligent, unmarried . . . But there was nothing of the old maid about her. Her figure, her posture, her attitude to him as a man, all suggested sexual awareness but she had a waspish tongue.

'You live near here?'

'A flat over the printing works. The foreman used to live there until he got married and needed a bigger place, then Uncle let me have it.'

'You live alone?'

A thin smile. 'Of course.'

'From your flat I suppose you can see the back of Benson's where Francis was killed.'

'If I look out of the right window.'

'Did you look out of the right window last night?'

'I didn't see Francis or anything happening to him if that's what you're getting at. In any case it was dark well before ten.'

'You didn't come to work by the way of the wharf walk this morning?'

'I never do.'

'Isn't it the quickest way?'

'Marginally, perhaps, but I always come by the street and pick up uncle's paper from the newsagent on my way.' She pointed to *The Times*, still neatly folded on her desk, and smiled: 'I still do it – force of habit, I suppose.' She crushed out the dog-end of her cigarette and turned towards him, perfectly composed.

'If the business had been shut down and the premises sold, what would have happened to you?'

She grimaced. 'It's not a question of what would have happened if, it's what *will* happen. I shall be out of a job and out of a home. Beryl won't keep the shop on. I suppose I shall get something in the way of redundancy pay but it won't amount to much.'

Wycliffe changed the subject. 'Your uncle died of a stroke?'

'Actually it was coronary thrombosis; he collapsed in his studio.'

'Studio?'

'My uncle used to paint, his studio is next door to this.'

'And he died there?'

'I found him when I came back from lunch. It looked as though he had collapsed while painting.' For the first time she showed emotion.

'Had he been ill?'

'He had high blood pressure and he suffered from

36

angina. It was made worse because he wouldn't do what the doctor told him. He was obstinate.'

'You were fond of him?'

She nodded.

'Presumably the doctor was satisfied that he died as a result of his illness?'

She looked at him oddly. 'Of course! The doctor issued a certificate which gave coronary thrombosis as the cause of death.'

'I'm sorry, but one has to ask these questions. Anyway, thank you for your help. Just one more thing: I would like a list of customers regularly visited by your cousin. Could you have it ready by this afternoon?'

She looked surprised but she agreed.

'Thank you. Now, perhaps, you will ask Miss Garland if she will see me.'

Miss Garland would.

The stairs and landing, lit by a murky skylight, were rarely cleaned, in sharp contrast with the office and shop. Beryl Garland was waiting for him on the landing, a lean, bony woman with uncared-for greying hair, a pallid complexion blotched with an unnatural pink, and restless suspicious eyes.

'Come into the living-room.'

The living-room had once been almost elegant: high, with a deep frieze, plaster cornice, and an elaborate ceiling rose, reminders of a time when even prosperous merchants lived over their shops. The window faced north across the harbour and the water, sparkling in the sunshine, made the room itself seem dark. The furniture was genteely shabby and not very clean. A black and white rough-haired terrier was asleep on the hearth rug.

'My friend, Miss Bond, Superintendent.'

Miss Bond, who was standing when he entered the

room, was the perfect complement to Beryl, plump instead of lean, dainty instead of gaunt, amiable instead of forbidding.

'We've known each other most of our lives and we were at school together, so we've no secrets.'

It dawned on Wycliffe that the room was smelling strongly of whisky, and that Miss Bond had probably hidden bottle and glasses while he was being received on the landing.

He was directed to a leather armchair by the empty fireplace while the two women seated themselves on dining chairs at the table. Their movements were deliberate and careful and Wycliffe had the impression of figures in slow motion, indeed of a whole existence that proceeded at a slower pace, muted, subdued, and infinitely depressing.

He expressed sympathy and it was received with complacency. 'My two closest relatives inside four days. Father died on Saturday of a coronary. Of course he's not been well for some time and he didn't take care of himself.' She lowered her voice. 'Blood pressure.' After a pause she went on: 'And angina; he was a difficult man! Wasn't he, Celia?'

Miss Bond shifted her position slightly and smiled but did not reply.

'I've given my life to looking after my father and my brother. I was thirty when mother died . . . Nobody can say I haven't done my duty.'

He led her to speak of her brother: 'I understand there is a daughter.'

'Ah! So they've told you that already. Francis was a young man when that happened and I can't see what it's got to do with this.'

'I believe the girl lives locally and that she has kept in touch with her father.'

'For what she could get! She and that boy were at the funeral yesterday. You never saw anything like it – the way they were dressed; and their hair! A disgrace! wasn't it, Celia?'

Miss Bond said: 'You know I wasn't there, dear.'

'No, well it was . . . At a funeral – it was an insult!'

For Beryl Garland the whole of reality was contained within the narrow horizons of her direct experience and her judgements were absolute.

'When was the last time you saw your brother, Miss Garland?'

'Yesterday evening at about nine o'clock. He was working in his room and I went in to tell him that I was going to spend the night with Miss Bond – I was upset, you understand. I came back at about eight this morning in time to get his breakfast and found the dog outside the back door, whining.'

'Has your brother seemed worried or nervous lately? Have you noticed any change in him?'

She shook her head with decision. 'No.'

'And last night when you spoke to him he was just as usual?'

'Just as usual, Superintendent.' She placed a bony hand firmly on the table top and fixed Wycliffe with her grey eyes. 'Francis was killed by hooligans. There's been a lot of that sort of thing in the town lately, and the police . . .' She decided not to finish that sentence.

Wycliffe said: 'But nothing was taken; his wallet, his money, his keys —'

She cut him short. 'Because the dog would have started to bark and frighten the ruffians off. That's what happened.' She turned to her friend. 'Miss Bond agrees with me, don't you Celia?'

Miss Bond nodded. 'It's true that there have been

39

several unpleasant incidents, mostly with young drunks.'

It was odd; Beryl's determination to convince him that her brother had been the victim of a random attack.

He was learning something of the dead man's background, admittedly from a biased witness, but any policeman knows that all witnesses are biased in some degree. He wanted to get the feel of the place, to find out what it was like to be Francis Garland, living with his father and sister in these rooms over the shop.

Beryl caught him looking at a painting hanging above the mantelpiece, a portrait of a middle-aged woman of exceptional beauty. 'My mother, just before she died at the age of fifty.' After a pause, she added in a church whisper: 'It was a growth – very quick.' She went on: 'Gifford Tate painted that. He was a great friend of my father's. Before Gifford had his stroke they used to go painting together all over the place. He's famous now, his pictures fetch thousands.'

Beryl having said her piece, silence took possession of the room; the two women sat, staring in front of them, scarcely moving a muscle. A trapped fly buzzed intermittently against the window panes and on the other side of the window the life of the harbour went on its unhurried way. The sounds from the street were muted.

Wycliffe, in the big black leather armchair by the empty grate, wondered if he was sitting in the old man's chair. Had Edwin spent idle hours in this room while his daughter made a great parade of doing the housework and kept up a running vituperative commentary on the last person or event to incur her displeasure? Or had he got the old man all wrong? He realised that he knew even less about the father than the son. He realised too that he needed to know about both. Father and son had died within a few days of each other . . .

Beryl broke the silence. 'I have to see father's lawyer this afteroon about the will. Of course Francis should have been there as well.' She looked down at her hands, resting on the table. 'I don't think Francis ever made a will so I suppose his share will come to me.' She shifted uneasily on her chair then, with a quick glance at Wycliffe: 'Is that right?'

'You will have to ask the solicitor about that, Miss Garland.'

'But you're a policeman; you must have some idea of the law. Celia thinks they'll say his illegitimate daughter is next-of-kin. That would be wicked! I mean, she's never done a hand's turn for her father or her grandfather —'

Miss Bond intervened. 'I really don't think the superintendent can help you, dear. You'll have to wait until you see Mr Shrimpton.'

Wycliffe said: 'Is he your father's solicitor?'

'Arthur Shrimpton, yes. The Shrimptons have looked after our affairs ever since my great grandfather started the business in 1900. In those days they lived next door but now they've only got their offices there. Over the bank.'

'Mr Shrimpton also acted for your brother?'

She looked at him in mild surprise at the question. 'Of course!'

Wycliffe said: 'I should like to see your brother's room, Miss Garland.'

'His room? What for?'

'In the circumstances the police need to know everything possible about your brother. It is one of the

41

ways in which we can hope to find out why he was killed.'

'I've told you why he was killed.'

Wycliffe's bland stare decided the issue. She got up from her chair. 'You'd better come with me.'

He followed her across the landing where she opened one of three doors. 'There you are!' Despite her pique about his refusal to discuss the will, she took a certain pride in showing him her brother's room. 'All these books . . . and a computer. Francis spent a lot of time in here studying. All about numbers.'

'Was he a mathematician?'

'Oh, no. He worked on numbers because he thought they controlled people's lives. More like astrology I think it was.'

Wycliffe walked over to the bookshelves. The books fell into two roughly equal groups: occult studies and lives of famous and infamous men and women through history. The occult section was dominated by works on numerology. He glanced over the titles: Gibson's *Science of Numerology*, Cheiro's *Book of Numbers*, Driver's *Sacred Numbers and Round Figures*, and perhaps 40 others. A good collection of scholarly nonsense.

He turned to the desk where there were several index cards in a little pile. Beryl was watching him with suspicious eyes. The cards were all concerned with Frederick the Great; the first, a sort of curriculum vitae, the others dealing with aspects of his character and the principal events in his life. Each entry was marked with a series of numbers. A nest of metal drawers contained several hundreds of such cards in which the lives of other distinguised men and women had been similarly dissected.

She asked: 'Do you understand it?'

'No.'

Beryl was smug. 'I didn't think you would.'

Wycliffe said: 'Did your brother go out much, apart from the travelling he did for the firm?'

'He took the dog for a walk every night.'

'Apart from that.'

'Apart from that he went out every Sunday after breakfast and he usually came back late. I've no idea where he went.'

'Presumably he had friends?'

'If he did he didn't tell me about them.'

'Didn't people come to see him, or telephone?'

'He sometimes had telephone calls but who from or what about I don't know. I don't listen at doors.' She added after a moment: 'I do know he wasn't liked; even as a boy he had no friends.' She said this with relish.

'Do you know if he had any contact with his relatives?'

She turned on him: 'Relatives?'

'I understand that you have an uncle and a cousin who live near the docks.'

'We don't acknowledge them!' Her contempt was regal. 'I'm sure he never went near them.'

'Just one more question: did your father or your brother own a gun of any sort?'

'A gun? Certainly not!'

'To your knowledge there has never been a gun in this house?'

'Never!'

He moved towards the door. 'I'm afraid we shall have to keep this room locked for a day or two.'

'*Locked*?'

'Until we've had a chance to go through his papers. It's quite usual; we shall try to cause as little trouble as possible.'

'It seems to me that it is we who are being treated like criminals but I don't suppose I have any choice.'

A final glance around the room, the books, the charts, the computer, the filing system . . . He had the impression of something out of key – not exactly false, but contrived. As though the setting was more important than the work.

He locked the door and slipped the key into his pocket. 'I assure you that we will add to your distress as little as possible, but we shall be here from time to time and you will also be asked to make a formal statement.' Impossible not to be pompous with this damned woman!

She looked at him with silent aggression and he left it at that. There were many questions he wanted to ask her but he needed ammunition.

She stood on the landing, watching him as he went down the stairs and out by the side door. He wondered if he would find anyone to grieve for either father or son.

As he passed the bank next door he noticed that it too had a side passage, but this one was decked out with tiles and had painted walls. A brass plate on the door, worn but shining, read: 'Shrimpton and Nicholls: Solicitors and Commissioners for Oaths.'

The street was slightly less congested, the time for unloading had passed and the lorries were gone. People ambled along, indulging in the local pastime of frustrating car drivers who had the temerity to attempt a breakthrough. Cars, of course, could and should have been excluded but that would have spoiled the fun.

Wycliffe had other preoccupations. A man of seventy-five dies of a heart condition and inside four days his son is shot dead. An actuary, assuming no casual connection, might calculate the odds against such a coincidence. Wycliffe thought they would be pretty high, so probability favoured a link. The most obvious one would be the will, but murder by advantaged legatees is a risky business. *Cui bono*? has a too obvious answer. All the same . . .

On the wharf activity was dying down. The body had been removed to the mortuary where Dr Franks would carry out the post mortem. A batch of film had gone for processing along with footprint casts and soil samples believed to be contaminated with blood or other tissue. Fox had found a bullet bedded in the ground and a cartridge case to go with it. It seemed that Francis had been shot with a self-loading pistol. a .32. They would know more when they had the report from Ballistics.

Now, one man was examining the steel tubes and struts of the scaffolding, dusting the surfaces with aluminium powder and squinting at the result through a lens; another was on his knees scrutinising the staging planks in case some fibres from the killer's clothing had become caught in the rough grain of the wood. Real Sherlock Holmes stuff! In reality, slow, monotonous, painstaking work which would almost certainly prove unrewarding.

'Check the register for licensed hand-guns of medium calibre.'

The headquarters team had arrived. Detective Inspector Kersey got out of one of the cars and came towards him. 'We're all here, sir. Lucy Lane is at the local nick taking over the paper work. Shaw is negotiating for that hen house over there.' Kersey pointed to a large portable building adjacent to the carpark. 'It seems a firm of accountants hired it as temporary accommodation while their offices were being refurbished and it's due to be removed. It would suit us better than one of our own mobile sardine cans.'

Kersey and Wycliffe had worked together for several years and their temperaments complemented each other. To Wycliffe's austere, almost puritanical approach, Kersey opposed an earthy realism and both were sufficiently tolerant to make the combination work.

'So, where do we go from here?'

'I'm going to take a look at the Garland printing works but I'll pick you up here in about half-an-hour and we'll go to lunch.'

Wycliffe had to make his way past a small crowd of would-be sightseers held well back by a uniformed policeman. A few yards off-shore several small craft provided others with vantage points but, as a spectacle, a scene of crime study ranks about level with a hole in the ground.

The printing works was a fairly modern concrete building with all the external charm of an army blockhouse, but the receptionist in the outer office was briskly efficient.

'I'll see if Mr Treloar is free.'

A brief exchange on the house telephone, a short delay, then Treloar joined them. A middle aged man in a grey overall, bald, very thin, with a conspicuous adam's apple; he walked with a limp. His manner was that of a man resigned to repeated interruptions: 'I suppose this is about Mr Francis; you'd better come into the office.'

The foreman's office was partitioned off from the shop floor and from it one could see the men at work on the machines – five or six of them – but part of the floor was screened off by large canvas sheets suspended from the roof trusses.

Treloar waved a despairing hand. 'It's chaos! We're having new photo typesetting equipment put in . . . A fine time for all this!'

His table was set out with batches of proof sheets clipped together, the ashtray was full of stubs, and there was a cup half full of coffee which looked as though it had gone cold hours before.

He drew up a chair for Wycliffe and sat down himself. 'I don't understand economics, Superintendent: why is it that in a country with three million on the dole some of us don't have time to breathe? Something wrong somewhere! Now, sir, how can I help you?'

Wycliffe said: 'Obviously you've heard about Francis Garland – how did you hear, by the way?'

'Cathy Carne rang me – sometime after nine.'

'The news came as a shock?'

Treloar brought out a packet of cigarettes, offered them to Wycliffe, then lit up himself. 'Not a shock exactly; a surprise, certainly.'

Obviously a man who chose his words with care.

'As far as you know did he have any enemies?'

'As far as I know he didn't have enemies or friends either, but I didn't know him very well.'

'You worked with him.'

A slow smile. 'You could say that. He spent three days a week here, more or less. I don't want to speak ill of the dead but as far as the work was concerned I have to say that he won't be missed.'

'What exactly did he do?'

'He saw commercial reps and talked to customers but he always called me in before he put in an order or gave an estimate.'

'So he knew his limitations.'

Treloar trickled smoke from between his lips. 'His father pointed them out to him often enough and he knew that things would drop on him from a great height if he put a foot wrong.'

'Edwin took an active part in the management here?'

A steady look from the grey eyes. 'He was the brains. I ran the place day to day, he decided policy. As long as you remembered that, everything was fine.'

'He came here often?'

'Every morning at half-past ten he would walk in through that door. He'd spend half-an-hour with me and another going round the machines, talking to the men. Apart from that he would be in touch by telephone.'

'You liked him?'

Hesitation. 'I admired him; he was a clever man and he was as good as his word. As to liking, I always had the feeling – I can't quite express it – the feeling that in his eyes I was all right – useful in fact, but that I didn't matter in myself. He had a way of looking at people as though they amused him, just like you might look at the antics of white mice in a cage. Sounds ridiculous, doesn't it?'

'Not to me.'

Treloar smoked for a while in silence, then he said: 'I suppose that was the man's nature but I've wondered sometimes whether it was why Francis turned out so bloody useless . . . if he was made to feel like that from childhood – insignificant, a bit of a joke.'

'What will happen now? Are you worried?'

Treloar pouted. 'Beryl will sell. As to being worried – no. I'm good at my job and anybody who wants to run this place would have to recognise the fact. Not that I welcome change; I was very satisfied as things were but it was obvious they wouldn't go on indefinitely.'

They chatted for a few minutes but Treloar had nothing more to say. One of his men was waiting to see him, there was a telephone call, a customer was asking for him, and the receptionist was getting agitated.

Wycliffe said: 'Just one more thing then I'll leave you to it. I understand Cathy Carne lives above this?'

'She has a flat up there but most of that floor is a store-room.'

'Surely she doesn't have to come through this lot to go to her flat?'

'Hardly! The flat is self-contained and there's an outside staircase on the other side of the building.'

Wycliffe thanked him and left. Outside he walked round the building. In the end facing the harbour steel doors stood open and he could see men at work inside, installing the new machines. The entrance to Cathy Carne's flat was around the corner – a wooden stairacse, well maintained, with a canopied landing at the top. He climbed the stairs but could see nothing through the hammered glass panels of the front door. The flat was at the quay end of the premises and from its windows there would be splendid views of the harbour, the waterfront, and the docks. It seemed that Cathy had a lot to lose through her uncle's death.

Brooding, Wycliffe walked back along the wharf to join Kersey in search of lunch.

Cathy Carne stood in the middle of the shop. It was a quiet time and Alice was re-stocking the shelves. Cathy stared into vacancy, seeing nothing. She was trying to grasp the radically changed situation with which she must come to terms. Edwin dead, Francis dead, and in such a short space of time. Four days ago in a similar quiet period she had been gossiping with her uncle, listening to his barbed comments on affairs, on the art world, and on his family. Now she was perplexed and afraid; perplexed because she did not understand what had happened, and afraid of what it might mean if she did.

She realised with a slight shock that she was staring straight at a man who was looking in through the shop window, staring back. It was Mark Garland of the excluded Garlands. She lifted a hand in acknowledgement, and this was all the encouragement he needed to come in.

Mark Garland was slight of build, very fair, good looking in a feminine way. He wore spectacles with thin gold rims which seemed to stress his femininity. Cathy had the impression that he was struggling to control extreme nervousness and his approach was absurdly tentative.

'I wondered whether to risk coming in or not. I didn't know what sort of reception I should get.'

Cathy was brusquely reassuring. 'There's no quarrel between us. Why should there be?'

'No, of course not! It's all very distressing. I'm very upset about Francis . . . more upset than I can say.'

Cathy waited for him to enlarge. He intrigued her, he was such a rabbit, yet Edwin had told her that he was subject to outbursts of violent temper.

'I wonder if you think I could have a word with Beryl? I would very much like to.' Another weak little smile. 'We haven't spoken since I was a child, Beryl and I. Absurd, isn't it?'

'There's no harm in trying; she won't eat you.'

'No . . . How should I go about it?'

'I'll call her if you like – or would you rather go up?'

He hesitated, looking round the shop as though it might help him to a decision. 'No, I'd rather you called her if you don't mind.'

Cathy went into the little hall and called up the stairs. Beryl's voice answered. 'What is it?'

'Mark Garland is here and he would like a word with you.'

50

'Well, I don't want a word with him. Nothing has changed; he needn't think it has; I don't want to hear or see anything of him or his father – ever. You can tell him that!' A door slammed upstairs.

Cathy returned to the shop. 'You heard? Sorry!'

He nodded, resigned. 'It's a pity . . . I was hoping to explain . . .' He went out of the shop, head bent, shoulders drooping.

Miss Bond had gone out to buy something simple for their lunch. 'A few sandwiches from Marks and Spencer, dear – but nothing with salmon. You know I daren't touch salmon.'

Beryl was restless and apprehensive, trying hard to find firm ground, and Mark Garland turning up like that had upset her. The gall of these people! Her feeling of insecurity had started some time before her father's death with a suspicion, soon amounting to certainty, that something was going on behind her back. It was mainly due to a subtle change in Francis. She had denied anything of the kind to the police but it was real enough. She knew him and his little moods so well: he had become more aggressive, more overtly secretive – and smug. When he was young he would say: 'I know something you don't!' Not so blatant now, but it meant the same.

And there was his behaviour since their father's death: odd little things she had scarcely noticed at the time but now they began to acquire significance in her mind. She glanced at the clock: five minutes to one. Soon Cathy Carne would be shutting shop to go to lunch. Beryl went downstairs and into the shop. Cathy was in the office.

'Anything I can do, Beryl?'

'No, I just wanted the key to father's studio.'

51

'But I haven't got it. If you remember, yesterday afternoon, after the funeral, Francis asked me to lock the studio and bring him the key. I did, and he put it on his ring.'

'Isn't there a spare?'

'Not as far as I know. Uncle always kept the studio locked and carried the key about with him.'

To this point Beryl's manner had been almost peremptory, now she became more relaxed and confiding. 'There's something I want to ask you, Cathy. When you came upstairs to say father had collapsed, didn't you think it was very odd, the way Francis rushed down without a word?'

Cathy was cautious. 'No, it didn't strike me like that. I thought he wanted to see if he could help his father, but it was too late.'

Beryl persisted. 'And when we came down together, after you'd telephoned Alan . . . You remember?'

There was a brief pause before Cathy replied. 'Yes, I remember. What about it?'

'You looked very puzzled about something. I saw you staring at Francis; I couldn't make it out.'

Cathy was dismissive. 'I don't know how I looked but I was shocked. We all were.'

Beryl lingered, her grey eyes fixed on Cathy for some time, then she said: 'I see. Well, you'll be wanting to go to your lunch. You'll be at Shrimpton's this afternoon?'

'Yes.'

'I suppose Alice is capable of looking after the shop?'

The first time Beryl had shown the slightest concern for the business. A straw in the wind?

Anna was in the kitchen preparing vegetables, and from where she stood at the sink she could look across the water to Falmouth, a few hundred yards away: the

Greenbank Hotel, the Royal Yacht Club, the new flats on the Packet Quays, then the backs of High Street and the pier. The narrow strip of water between was dotted with small craft of every description, all facing upstream. The sun shone and everywhere there was stillness. Life seemed suspended and she had a disquieting sense of being quite alone. She switched on the radio to recover normality.

Her grandfather's death had affected her more than she would have thought possible. She had heard the news with regret, with sadness, but hardly with grief. After all, old men die. A month ago he had come to see her and now she understood for the first time that what he had said to her then would change her life. At the funeral (she had never been to a funeral before) it had come to her quite suddenly that something was ending in herself, that she was being challenged to take hold of her life, to make decisions, and she had quarrelled with Terry because of it.

The front door opened then slammed. Her mother had been to Falmouth shopping. She was back early. She burst into the kitchen, two shopping bags in one hand and one in the other.

'You're early.'

Freda dropped her bags and slumped on a chair. She was flushed and breathing hard. 'I got the first ferry I could after I heard . . . Shut that damn thing off, Anna!'

Anna switched off the radio.

In the silence she could hear her mother wheezing as she breathed. Freda was grossly overweight. An elaborately floral dress exposed great volumes of lobster-coloured flesh.

'What did you hear?' Anna was accustomed to her mother's histrionics.

'It's about your father.'

'What about him?'

'He's dead, Anna – murdered.'

Anna stood motionless, potato in one hand, knife in the other. There was nothing she could say, nothing she could think because she felt nothing. Only in her mind's eye she saw the image of her father, rather big, fleshy, with bulging expressionless eyes.

'The police are all over the place. I thought they might have got here before I did.'

Anna said nothing.

'He was shot last night when he was taking the dog for a walk.'

'Shot? On the wharf?'

'Yes.'

'Do they know who did it?'

'How should I know?'

Anna picked up the saucepan into which she had been putting potatoes and transferred it to the stove. Her mother watched her.

'In some ways you're just like your father, Anna. You never *feel* anything. You're cold inside!' Freda started to unpack her shopping. At one of the cupboards, with her back to the room she said: 'Terry didn't come home last night.'

Anna said nothing.

'Have you seen him this morning?'

'No.'

'What happened?'

'We had a row.'

'What about?'

'Nothing – everything. I was fed up.'

'Where would he sleep?'

'In the van, I suppose. He's done it often enough before.'

She was thinking of the periodic visits she had made to her father; they were all the same; their conversations could have been scripted:

'How is your mother?'

'All right.'

'And you?'

'I'm all right.'

'Good!' Then when the silence became uncomfortable he would reach into his pocket for his wallet. 'There, now! Buy yourself something.' He thought it was what she had come for. Perhaps he was right . . . Yet there must have been something more. Now he was dead.

Anna started to slice up runner beans. Freda said: 'You'll still go to the lawyer's this afternoon?'

'I suppose so.'

'Your grandfather thought a lot of you. He remembered you every Christmas and birthday . . . He must have left you something and you might as well know what.'

There was a knock at the front door. Freda said: 'There they are! The police.'

CHAPTER THREE

Wycliffe was watching two men in a rowing boat. One rowed while the other held a rope over the stern. They would row about fifty yards in one direction, then turn round and row back, seemingly over the same ground. What were they doing? Were they trawling for something? A lost moorings, perhaps? That was the trouble with harbour-watching, there were so many inexplicable activities carried on at a stately pace and with the deliberation of a choreographed performance.

The team had acquired the use of the large Portakabin recently occupied by a firm of accountants while their offices were being refurbished. Although all fittings and furniture had been removed it was Ritzy accommodation compared to a mobile incident van or the decayed huts and barn-like halls to which they were accustomed. There was even a screened-off cubicle which could be used as an interview room. More to the point, it was next door to the car-park and overlooked the harbour within two hundred yards of the Garlands' shop. A pantechnicon from central stores had delivered the official ration of battered furniture and a communications unit with office equipment, stationery and the basic materials for preparing police tea. A large-scale map was pinned to one wall and there was a blackboard for briefings.

By mid-afternoon they were in business.

Uniformed men and Wycliffe's detective constables

were questioning the very few people who actually lived in the street. Publicans whose premises backed on the harbour were interviewed and, over local radio, people were being asked to come forward if they had been in the neighbourhood the night before, especially those who had used the car-park. It was quite possible that the killer had come and gone by car. On the assumption that he or she might not have carried the murder weapon away Wycliffe had ordered a search of the foreshore, and a police frogman was floundering about in the shallow off-shore waters like a porpoise on the point of stranding.

'The dead man spent two days a week travelling for the firm, taking orders and delivering goods. I will let you have a list of his customers and I want them contacted, in the first instance by telephone. Find out when he last called and try to get an impression of what they thought of him. Get them to talk, and if there is a hint of anything unusual report to me.' Kersey, briefing his troops.

'We also want to know exactly how Garland spent his time from Saturday afternoon when his father died to last night when somebody shot him on the wharf. I shall draw up a timetable, hour by hour, and allowing for the fact that he must have slept, I expect to see the spaces filled in.

'The shot that killed Garland was fired at a few minutes past ten. Most of the people who were in the street at that time would have been in one or other of the pubs, but don't forget that the harbour is full of craft of all sorts and there are sure to have been people aboard some of them.'

Wycliffe dealt with the media. Interest was minimal; the fatal shooting of a small-town shopkeeper wouldn't make much of a splash, the ripples would scarcely extend to the National dailies.

Wycliffe's table was placed against the row of windows at one end of the temporary building. He had the pathologist's preliminary report which had been dictated over the telephone. 'A single wound of entry situated in the right parietal bone just anterior to the lambdoid suture and close to the saggital suture. The nature of the wound suggests a bullet of medium calibre fired at close range, under 60 centimetres. The bullet traversed the skull and was deflected in its passage to emerge on the left side, shattering bones in the area of articulation of the lower jaw.

'This would be consistent with the victim having been shot from above and slightly behind. Death must have been instantaneous.

'The facial bruising was caused 24-36 hours before death and is typical of injury brought about by a blow from a human fist.'

Already officers were returning from enquiries with completed interview-forms and Lucy Lane was going through them as they came in. Kersey was briefing himself from the paperwork so far.

Detective Sergeant Lucy Lane was still well under thirty. A good school record; university. Then what? Something constructive – working with people. But having no wish, as Virginia Woolf put it, 'to dabble her fingers self-approvingly in the stuff of other souls' and believing in the stick and carrot philosophy of human conduct, she joined the police. Oddly, her outlook was more authoritarian than her chief's. After thirty years in the force Wycliffe still held fast to a lingering hope that man may yet prove perfectable; woman too. Lucy, probably influenced by her parson father, was more inclined to a belief in original sin.

'Look at this, sir.' She passed over two reports with items marked in red.

The first concerned the landlord's wife at the Packet Inn. At about ten-fifteen the previous evening she had heard a 'crack' followed by a dog barking – yapping, she said. It had gone on for some time, she couldn't say how long. She was busy serving and really didn't think much about it.

The other report was from the DC who had called on Garland's daughter, Anna, and her mother. They had already heard the news and seemed to take it calmly. The officer had not seen the girl's boyfriend and was told that they did not know where he was.

'So?' Wycliffe returned the sheets.

'Just that Sergeant Shaw checked with Records. This young man, Terrence John Gill, has a conviction. Two years ago he was convicted of causing a breach of the peace at St Mawgan airfield during a CND demo.'

'What happened in court?'

'He was bound over.'

'I don't suppose that makes him a potential killer but we need to find him. Put somebody on to it.'

He thought of Beryl and the need to come to grips with the Garland set-up as it had been before the old man's death. Beryl needed firm handling but losing father and brother inside four days must mean something more than the prospect of a secure income. Lucy Lane with her stick and carrot philosophy might be the best one to deal with her.

'I want you to talk to Beryl Garland. We want background. We also want her formal statement. Take a DC with you and get started on turning over Francis's room. On second thoughts, take Shaw and see what he can make of that computer thing.'

Wycliffe had little patience with and no interest in technological gadgetry. He believed that the human capacity for moral, social, and political adaptation had been stretched to its limit in the first century of the Industrial Revolution and fatally outstripped since.

'Will we be looking for anything in particular, sir?'

'Use your imagination. Whatever Beryl believes or pretends to believe about her brother being mugged, he was in fact deliberately murdered by someone lying in wait for him on the scaffolding. There must have been an involvement in something sufficiently profitable or menacing or both to lead somebody to murder. I've got an appointment with Shrimpton, the lawyer, at four and I shall look in at the shop afterwards.'

He arrived on time for his appointment and he was not kept waiting; the receptionist introduced him at once.

Shrimpton was in the mid-forties, overweight, and slightly larger than life, a sociable type. His skin was bronzed, his thinning hair was bleached by sun and sea, and Wycliffe felt sure that he spent as little time as possible away from boats, the sea, and the club bar. Of course his office overlooked the harbour and was hung with enlarged photographs of yachts and of sailing occasions.

'Smoke? . . . I will if you don't mind.' He lit a small cigar. 'I know why you're here and I might tell you I've had one hell of an afternoon.' He blew out a cloud of smoke. 'I suppose you know our Beryl?'

'I've spoken to her briefly.'

'Then you know her. Edwin was a crafty old so-and-so and he didn't like his children very much – not that I blame him – so I thought I'd better get the beneficiaries together and explain. We had a date for this afternoon but when I heard about Francis it seemed the decent thing to postpone the arrangement. I rang Beryl with condolences and the suggestion that we should meet later in the week. Not on your life! You'd think I was proposing to give away her share to a cats' home. So we went ahead as planned: Beryl, Cathy Carne – you've met Cathy? Great girl! Anna – Francis's side-kick – Alan Tate and Mike Treloar, the foreman at the printing works. Of course Francis should have been with us.'

Wycliffe said: 'Alan Tate?'

'Gifford Tate's son. Gifford and old Edwin were life-long buddies. Alan is a doctor and he lives with his stepmother in the family house – up the hill towards Wood Lane.'

'And Alan Tate is a beneficiary under the will?'

'In a small way.' He broke off, staring out of the window. 'See that?'

A heavily built boat, painted slate-blue, cutter rigged, was gliding downstream. 'That's one of the Falmouth Quay Punts. She's at least eighty years old, of course she's been restored. Before the days of radio, boats like her would race down-channel as far as the Lizard to get first contact for the ship-to-shore trade from vessels making port. Wonderful craft! I envy old Podgy Hicks that boat.

'But perhaps you're not addicted.' Reluctantly he brought his attention back to business. 'Yes, well, Edwin's testament.' He glanced at the document in front of him. 'The will was made about a year ago and this is what it amounts to: "The shop premises and stock and all assets pertaining to the business together with the contents of my studio excepting only my tube of Winsor blue to my niece and dear friend Cathy Carne".'

Shrimpton looked up. 'You can imagine how that ruffled Beryl's feathers! For a moment I thought she was going the same way as her father. Then, £10,000 to

61

Anna, £5,000 to Mike Treloar, and £1,000 to Alan Tate – "the son of my friend Gifford Tate together with my tube of Winsor blue" —'

'What's all this about Winsor blue? It sounds like a butterfly.'

Shrimpton grinned. 'One of the old man's little jokes. Typical! As I said, Gifford Tate and he were buddies, and it was some argument they had about colours. Winsor blue is a colour used by painters. Of course old man Tate died years ago.

'There's another legacy of £1,000, this time to his friend Martin Burger, "more than enough for that new pair of spectacles which I hope may improve his judgement and help him to see the obvious." Burger wasn't here this afternoon; he's a bit doddery on his legs and doesn't get about much.

'Anyway, the printing works and the business associated with it together with the residue of the estate after discharge of all debts and liabilities are left jointly to Beryl and Francis. That's it.'

'Is the residue going to amount to much?'

'I wouldn't mind it coming my way. Edwin owned the freehold of another property in the street, let on a fat lease, there is more property on the sea-front, and a nice carefully nurtured portfolio of equities. The Garlands have been in this game for eighty years – accumulating, not spending. Edwin liked to pretend that the art business and the printing were his livelihood, in fact they probably represent less than half his assets.'

'Isn't it a bit odd to leave property to joint heirs with no conditions laid down for its distribution?'

Shrimpton nodded. 'I tried to persuade him out of it but he wouldn't budge. A recipe for in-fighting that's what it is, and that's what the old devil intended, although he wouldn't admit it. I think he saw himself, sitting up there, watching the fun. Of course now it's going to be a damn sight funnier than even he imagined.'

'How come? With Francis out of the way —'

Shrimpton tapped ash off his cigar. 'With Francis out of the way Beryl will have to come to terms with his heir and to the best of my belief Francis never made a will. He meant to. He was in this office a fortnight ago saying that it was about time as his father was getting on and one never knew, et cetera et cetera . . . He promised to bring me a few notes from which I could prepare a draft but he never did.'

'So?'

'You know the answer to that, and so does Beryl now, though I wrapped it up a bit to save her having a fit on the spot. Young Anna is going to be well heeled but she will have to come to some arrangement with Beryl and Beryl would prefer, much, to deal with the devil himself. If the old man really is up there watching he's in for some good laughs.'

'What was Anna's reaction?'

Shrimpton grimaced. 'Hard to tell. I half thought the implications of Francis's death hadn't got through to her, but that girl doesn't give much away.'

'How did Cathy Carne receive her bit of glad news? Do you think it was a complete surprise?'

Shrimpton was emphatic. 'I'm certain! I've never seen anyone so astonished unless it was dear Beryl. I can't imagine what Francis's reaction would have been. I can't help being thankful I didn't have to cope with it. Incidentally, the old man wrote Cathy a letter which I was charged to pass over unopened. And one other thing you should know for the record: Jimmy Rowe, the old man's accountant, and I are joint executors, God help us!'

Wycliffe was grateful and said so. 'Now I'm going to ask you to be indiscreet. If Francis had made a will have you any idea how it would have gone?'

Shrimpton threw away the stub of his cigar. 'You are asking me to be clairvoyant as well as indiscreet. Francis told me nothing of his intentions so I can only guess.'

'And?'

A broad grin. 'You know nothing of any woman in his life?'

'Nothing. Was there one?'

'I'm not sure, but from things he let drop from time to time I think there probably was. Once or twice lately he's mentioned the possibility that he might "change his way of life" which could mean that he intended to get married, but with Francis it could equally mean that he was thinking of taking up golf or ludo.'

'I gather you were not fond of him.'

'I was not. I went to school with Francis and he was always odd man out. He wasn't very bright and he was more than a bit of a bore with it.'

'A couple of adjectives to describe him?'

Shrimpton laughed outright. 'You're a bloody old copper, I must say! Well, it can't do him any harm where he's gone. Two adjectives . . . devious is one, he was certainly that; and I'm afraid the other would have to be spiteful. You can add secretive for good measure though he hadn't much to be secretive about.'

'Somebody killed him.'

'Yes, and I must admit that surprises me. Francis could have been involved in something a bit shady but nothing that would have brought him within range of any violence. He was a timid soul.'

'One more question, then I won't bother you any

more. Can you tell me about the Garland relatives – Thomas's side of the family?'

'Not a lot. Thomas was a younger son and it seems he had no interest in the business; he went to university and became a teacher. At some stage he came back to Cornwall and taught. His son, Mark, trained as an osteopath or something and set up in practice here. Thomas's wife died and he and Mark continued to live in the family house down by the railway station.

'The trouble began when grandather Garland died about thirty years ago – in my father's time – and left almost everything to Edwin. Thomas felt hard done by, contested the will and lost. I don't think the two sides of the family have had anything to do with each other since.'

They parted on the best of terms. Shrimpton came with him to the top of the stairs. 'If you fancy a bit of sailing while you're here you know where to come.'

Wycliffe was anxious to talk to Cathy Carne again. Since his meeting with her that morning she had learned that she would become the owner of the business and premises. If the news was really unexpected she would be off balance and it is at such times that people are most likely to speak the truth.

As he entered the shop the young girl assistant came forward; she recognised him at once. 'Miss Carne is in the office.'

He went through and tapped on the office door.

A listless 'Come in!'

He found her sitting at the desk which was quite clear. 'Oh, it's you. I let your inspector have the list of Francis's customers you asked for.' She drummed on the desk with her fingers. 'I suppose you've heard?'

'I've just left Shrimpton. Was it totally unexpected?'

She turned on him irritably. 'Of course it was unexpected! What the hell do you think? I'd hoped for a little money, at the very most, a thousand. I can't take it in. I should be over the moon; instead . . .'

'What about Beryl?'

She reached for her cigarettes. 'Yes. What about Beryl? You may well ask. She's moving in with Celia Bond at the end of the month – or so she says. I told her she's welcome to stay up there just as long as she wants and what she said wouldn't bear repeating. I feel guilty, though God knows why I should. I've put more into this place than she and her brother together; a damn sight more!' She lit a cigarette and smoked in short, angry puffs.

Wycliffe sat down without being invited. 'My people are upstairs talking to Beryl and going through Francis's room, looking for anything which might explain why he was murdered. In my own mind I can't separate his death from his father's.'

She looked at him sharply. 'You're not suggesting —'

'That your uncle was murdered? No, merely that there is some sort of connection. He died in his studio; did he spend much time there?'

'A great deal.'

'Doing what?'

'Well, for one thing he did all our framing and there's quite a lot of that, but he painted too.'

'Did he sell his pictures?'

'Oh, yes. A number were sold through the shop though he would never have them put on display; others went to shops and commercial galleries in this part of the world. Of course he never made a name for himself, like Gifford Tate, though Tate himself reckoned uncle was the better painter. They were great friends – there were three of them: Uncle, Gifford

Tate, and Papa Burger – I don't know why "papa" but they always called him that. He had money and was always a bit of a dilettante. They used to go off painting together at week-ends, often in Burger's boat, and they spent quite long holidays abroad. Of course Tate died seven or eight years ago. In his will he appointed Uncle Edwin as his art executor.

'Incidentally there's an exhibition of Tate's work starting in the town next week. After that it goes on tour: Plymouth, Cardiff, London, Newcastle and Glasgow. A big affair. Uncle was really responsible for getting it organised – sponsorship and so forth. He was really looking forward to that exhibition.'

'And Burger?'

'Oh, Papa is still living up at Wood Lane. Didn't Shrimpton tell you. Uncle left him £1,000 to buy a pair of spectacles? A joke, of course. He's lost the use of his legs and doesn't get about much but Uncle went to see him two or three times a week.'

'What do you know about Winsor blue?'

She laughed, the tension suddenly released, and it occurred to Wycliffe that she was very attractive when she laughed. 'It's another joke they had, like Papa Burger and the spectacles. Winsor blue is a trade mark for an artists' colour which was first marketed sometime in the thirties. Gifford Tate started to use it as soon as it came out, he reckoned it brought him luck. Uncle used to tease him about it and it became a standing joke.'

'So leaving Alan Tate a tube of Winsor blue —'

'I suppose it was a way of wishing him luck.'

'Alan Tate is a doctor?'

'That's right. He was Uncle's doctor. Mine too, for that matter.'

'Did he issue the death certificate?'

'Of course!'

Wycliffe was impressed by her seemingly transparent honesty and by her spontaneity that had something refreshingly youthful about it. He could understand Edwin entrusting her with his business.

'I believe your uncle left a letter for you.'

'Yes.' The shutters came down.

'You've read it?'

'Yes; and destroyed it as he asked me to do.'

'You were in a hurry.'

'I did what I was asked to do.'

'Are you prepared to tell me what was in it?'

She hesitated. 'It gave me some advice about dealing with problems which might arise.'

'With the family?'

'Yes, and that is all I am prepared to say.'

'Just one more thing: what exactly was Francis doing with his books, his filing system and his computer?'

'I suppose the short answer would be, conning himself. In a burst of confidence one day he told me that he was working out a new system of numerology, developed from a study of people whose lives have been well documented. His father used to say that he was so desperately anxious to amount to something that he chose a subject about which critical people knew nothing and cared less.'

'Sounds a bit harsh.'

'Uncle didn't suffer fools gladly.'

Wycliffe stood up. 'Thanks for your help. I want a word with my people upstairs.'

As he was leaving the office he stopped by another door. 'The studio?'

'Yes, I'm afraid it's locked and Francis had the key.'

'It doesn't matter. I expect we shall come across it.'

He went upstairs. After the crisp freshness of the

shop, the flat had a musty stale smell. Edwin must have been struck by the contrast each time he climbed the stairs.

Lucy Lane and Shaw were at work in Francis's room which overlooked the street. The shops were closing and there was that burst of activity before things settled down to the evening calm. Lucy Lane was sitting at the desk, turning the pages of a loose-leaf manuscript file. She looked like a schoolgirl doing her homework. By contrast, Shaw, communing with the computer and making a new friend, looked like one of those whiz-kids who, from their glass and concrete towers, manipulate the world's money markets. It sometimes came as a slight shock to Wycliffe to have this paragon of the modern virtues working under his direction.

He said: 'Anything for me?'

Lucy Lane answered: 'He was writing a book on numerology. To me it's all gobbledegook, but here's the title.'

She held out the first page of the manuscript file for him to read. It was written in a careful script, meticulously spaced: 'A New System of Numerology by Francis Garland.' And there followed a paragraph in smaller script: 'Derived by the inductive method from studies of the lives of famous and infamous men and women, past and present, and including a new Universal Alphabet which disposes of the conflict between the "Hebrew" and the "Modern" systems.'

Wycliffe said: 'You need a dedication to a Noble Lord to go with that.'

Lucy Lane laughed. 'Quarto, with fine portrait vignette on title. Bound in contemporary calf . . .' She closed the file and put it aside. 'He also kept a diary of sorts though most of the entries don't tell you much.' She picked up a hard-covered exercise book. 'It looks as though he had a woman friend; he refers to her as "M". She's mentioned frequently but he never gives any clue as to who she is or the nature of their relationship.'

Wycliffe said: 'The lawyer thought there was a woman but he had no idea who she might be. We must try to find out. Anything else?'

'There's an earlier entry about his father.' She turned back through the pages. 'It's dated July 15th – just over a year ago – and he writes: "Today father told me something about himself which I can scarcely believe. It's incredible to think that it's been going on all these years! And when I asked him what would happen if it got known he just smiled and said I could talk if I wanted to. But why tell me? And why now?"'

'Dramatic! What do you make of it?'

Lucy Lane sucked the top of her ball-point. Meditative. 'A man of seventy-five, a widower, well off – what secrets would a man like that be likely to have? I mean, what would make him vulnerable? Unless he was keen on little boys or little girls. . . .'

'Talk to Beryl. She probably won't tell you anything but you may be able to judge whether she knows anything, and if she does, the sort of area we are in.'

He turned to Shaw who had not ceased his manipulations of the keyboard. 'And the oracle?'

Shaw said: 'It's difficult to work out his programme but it seems that he analysed his subjects and classified their attributes, their doings, and the major events in their lives by coded numbers. He used the computer to establish correlations. That's about as far as I've got.'

'Don't spend to much time on it unless it seems to have more relevanace to the case. Any correspondence?'

Lucy Lane said: 'There's a drawer full of letters all

70

jumbled together; we haven't got round to them yet.'

He decided to leave them to it, and as he came out on the landing he almost collided with Beryl who must have been eavesdropping. She was flushed, her eyes were moist and her hair was wild.

She attacked at once: 'I suppose she's told you that this is no longer my home so you think you can come and go as you please. Well, I shall move out when it suits me but I want you to know that the *contents* of these rooms are mine and I shall fight for them in Court if need be.'

Wycliffe felt sorry for her; self-centred and cantankerous as she was, she had suffered some shocks. 'I merely wanted a word with my people who are working on your brother's papers.'

Beryl made a derisive sound. 'That girl of yours asked me for a statement and I gave her one – more than she bargained for, and I made her take it all down.'

'I would like to ask you one or two more questions if I may.'

She was about to refuse but thought better of it. 'You'd better come in here.'

He followed her into the living-room but she did not ask him to sit down. 'Well?'

'In your brother's papers there is mention of something your father told him about a year ago which greatly surprised and puzzled him. From the context it is clear that the secret, whatever it was, was of long standing.'

He saw the change in her expression; antagonism replaced by . . . by fear? Was that too strong? At any rate she cut him short: 'Are you saying that my father had a shameful secret of some sort?'

'No, I am not; merely that there was something he

71

had previously kept to himself which he confided to your brother. I am wondering if you have any idea of what it could be?'

Beryl was staring at him, her lips were trembling and it was clear that she was deeply disturbed. In the end she said: 'This is all nonsense! Wicked nonsense! Francis was a fool!'

'So you know of nothing which your father might have confided to Francis which would greatly disturb him?'

'Of course I know of nothing! Francis was always stirring, trying to score off people . . .' She broke off, on the verge of tears.

Impossible to judge whether she knew or did not know whatever it was that Francis had been told, and there was nothing to be gained by turning the screw too hard.

'Have you noticed any change in your brother recently – say in the last few months? Any change in his relations with his father?'

'I've noticed nothing and I certainly would have if there was anything to notice!'

Back in the street workmen were stretching a banner between the shops above the traffic: 'The Gifford Tate Exhibition of Paintings; Open 11th–22nd August. Admission Free.'

Wycliffe felt that he was getting to know the people who had been closest to the dead man. Eight hours ago he had never heard of any of them, now he was thinking of them by their first names: Francis, Edwin, Beryl, Anna, Cathy . . . And he was able to fit a face and provisionally a temperament to four of them. Francis Garland was the victim and therefore the central figure in the case. Always start with the victim and try to trace around him the web of relationships in which he was involved. That was how he worked, but in this case he could not free himself of the notion that although Francis was the victim he might not be the central figure. His father seemed a more promising candidate for that role and he had died a natural death. Did that mean that the murder was . . . was peripheral?

He promised himself that he would devote at least as much attention to the father as to the son.

CHAPTER FOUR

'What do you want me for?'

'Where did you sleep last night?'

'In my van.'

'On this car-park?'

'Yes.'

'Do you usually spend your nights in the back of your van?'

'No. I live with my girlfriend and her mother in Flushing.'

'So why weren't you there last night?'

'We had a row.'

'About what?'

'God knows! What are rows usually about?'

'Money in my experience.'

Once it was known that Terry Gill was wanted for questioning, a young constable who knew him, all bright eyed and bushy tailed, pointed out that his van had been parked in the car-park all day within fifty yards of the Incident Room.

'I know him, sir. We keep an eye on him.'

So all they had needed to do was wait and, at five o'clock, the wanted man had turned up. Now he was being interrogated by Kersey in the make-shift interview room.

'Where have you been all day?'

'In Redruth to see an old mate of mine.'

'How did you get there without the van?'

'By bus. My dynamo has been dodgy and it finally packed up. I was short of a few quid to do anything about it so my mate lent me the money, we went to a scrap yard, picked up a spare and he delivered me back here in his motor, then your chaps picked me up.'

'What time did you leave this morning?'

'Early. Sevenish. I couldn't sleep so I thought I might as well get going.'

For all his long hair, bandeau and earrings which made him look like a weedy Viking, Terry Gill was a very ordinary young man, and pathetic; pathetic because he so obviously wanted to amount to something and had no idea what. Kersey would have written him off as harmless had it not been for his extreme wariness. Each question seemed to come as a relief, as though he had expected something more dangerous.

'So last night at, say, ten o'clock, where were you?'

'In my van, I expect. I'm not very good on time.'

At that point, Wycliffe joined them. Kersey looked up. 'This is Terry Gill, sir, Anna's boyfriend. He's telling us how he spent last night here, on the car-park, in his van.'

'So if you were in your van you couldn't have been two hundred yards away on the scaffolding behind Benson's furniture shop?'

This was the bull's eye. The boy looked from one to the other of them and it was a moment or two before he could find his voice, then: 'I don't know what you mean.'

'What are you so frightened of?'

'I'm not frightened.'

'You could have fooled me.' Kersey leaned forward across the table, his rubbery features close to the boy. 'Look, sonny, it sticks out a mile that you want to get something off your chest but you're scared to hell what will happen to you if you do. All I can say is the longer you mess me about the worse it will get. Now let's be serious. Take it a step at a time. When did you last see your girlfriend's father?'

'At the old man's funeral yesterday. He came and spoke to us – to Anna and me.'

'What did he say?'

'He was very friendly and nice; he wanted to know if Anna had been asked to come to the lawyer's about her grandfather's will.' Terry was recovering his voice if not his composure.

'And had she?'

'Yes.'

'So she had expectations.'

'Of something, I suppose.'

'Is that what you quarrelled about?'

'I don't think so. She was very queer after the funeral. I couldn't make her out.'

Wycliffe said: 'Anna's share in her grandfather's will was £10,000.'

The boy looked amazed. 'That's money! I don't think she was expecting anything like that.'

'But now she will get a lot more than that.'

'More?'

'From her father. It seems he didn't make a will and if that's the case Anna will get his share.'

'But her father isn't dead.' The words were spoken mechanically as though by a bad actor.

Kersey cut in. 'But he is, you know. Somebody shot him by the scaffolding behind Benson's just after ten last night.' Kersey's face split into a grin that would have intimidated a gorilla. 'So that brings us back to where we started.'

'You mean he was murdered?' Weakly.

'I mean he was murdered. As if you didn't know!'

'You don't think I . . . I mean, if I'd had anything to do with it do you think I'd have left my van here and come back —'

Kersey cut him short. 'Killers are usually stupid but some people might think it was a clever move to do just that. Did you know that Garland took his dog for a walk along the wharf every night?'

'No – yes.'

'We takes our choice. And you ask us to believe that out of a dozen car-parks and hundreds of side streets you could have chosen you picked this place by chance? Try telling that to your lawyer.'

'My God, I didn't kill him!'

'No? So what did you do?'

The boy paused and seemed to be gathering his wits. 'I admit I wanted to speak to him.'

'What about?'

He hesitated. 'We had that row – Anna and me. She said there was no future for us; me with no proper job and no prospects.'

'Well?'

'There's a cottage with three acres going on the Helston road. I know about market gardening and I could make a go of that. Vegetables for the health shop market, organically grown – that sort of thing.' He looked dubiously at Kersey as though he feared the very idea might provoke him to violence.

'And you thought your girl's father might put up the money?'

'As a loan – an investment.'

'Why not go and see him in the proper way instead of lurking around by night?'

He shook his head. 'I couldn't face Anna's aunt Beryl – she hates me – or Cathy Carne either, for that matter.'

77

'So what happened?'

'I saw him as he was crossing the car-park with his dog.' He was silent for a while and they could hear someone on the telephone in the main room.

Kersey prompted him: 'And?'

'I followed him some way behind.'

'How far?'

'To just past Spargo's; I couldn't raise the nerve to catch him up and speak to him. All of a sudden it seemed to be the wrong time and the wrong way to go about it, what with it being the day of the old man's funeral and everything . . . I decided after all it would be better to go and see him in the shop like you said—'

'If you got as far as Spargo's you must have seen him go under the scaffolding.'

'No, I didn't. I was some way behind, it was misty, and when I got there I couldn't see him. Then, all of a sudden, there was a sort of bang and the dog started yelping and I thought he must have fallen or something and that he might be hurt. I started running and when I reached this end of the scaffolding I saw a woman bending over something on the ground at the other end. I think she must have heard me because she ran off like the clappers towards the quay.'

'You said a woman.'

'I thought it was a woman at the time. Of course I could be wrong I suppose.'

'Wearing a skirt or trousers?'

'Oh, not a skirt – jeans I thought.'

'Thin or fat?'

'Not fat, definitely.'

'Short or tall?'

Time to ponder, then: 'Medium height, perhaps on the tall side for a woman.'

'Was he or she carrying anything?'

'Not that I could see.'

The questions were pressed but they could get nothing more definite: 'It looked like a woman.'

'Go on.'

He drew a deep breath. 'I went to look and though it was pretty dark I could see enough. It made me want to throw up. I wanted to get out. I went back to the van and the bloody thing wouldn't start so I waited there till morning when I could catch a bus and . . . and, well, just get out.'

At last he was packed off to sub-division: held for questioning.

Wycliffe said: 'Before we have to turn him loose – which we shall, get Lucy Lane over to Flushing to talk to the girl.'

Wycliffe drove the sixty miles home to another estuary while his team was given lodgings in the town.

The Wycliffes lived in The Watch House, a former coast-guard property overlooking the narrows on the Cornish side. They had a half-acre of garden, which Helen had planned and sedulously cultivated with shrubs and trees, and a plot for vegetables and fruit. Only a little-used footpath separated their garden from the shore.

He pulled into his drive as the church clock at St Juliot was striking eight; a perfect summer evening with the waters of the estuary a mirror to the sky. Helen was in the kitchen preparing a sweet savour as an offering to her lord.

'How did the inspection go?'

'It didn't. I'm on a case.'

'I know; I heard on the radio. You can pour me a sherry.'

'What are we eating?'

'I intended a salad but I thought you might have missed out on lunch so we've got grilled lamb chops with minted potatoes and glazed carrots.'

'Smells nice.'

They sipped their sherry while Helen prepared a fresh fruit salad.

Wycliffe said: 'What do you know about Gifford Tate?'

'The painter? I know that he's dead, that he lived somewhere in West Cornwall, that his pictures are making high prices and that I wish we could afford one. I've got a catalogue of an exhibition of his somewhere and I'll look it out if you're interested. Come to think of it, I remember reading something recently about a new exhibition of his, going on tour. How's that?'

'All right for a start. Now try Edwin Garland.'

Helen frowned and pushed back the hair from her forehead, a habit she had when thinking. 'I've heard the name. Was he a painter too?'

'Was is the operative word: he died last Saturday.'

'Not murdered?'

'No, that distinction was reserved for his son. It seems that Garland and Tate were buddies in their day.'

'I'll see what I can find after we've eaten.'

The french windows of the living-room stood open while they ate and by the time they reached the coffee stage darkness had closed over the hills across the water.

'I'll get that catalogue.'

Helen was not long gone: she had a filing system which covered the composers and the painters she enjoyed. 'Here we are: retrospective at the Hayward in 1976.'

The catalogue was a glossy production with several

illustrations in colour and black-and-white. Wycliffe turned the pages. There was the usual synoptic paragraph or two: 'Born Egham 1907; studied at the Slade Schools . . . Moved to Cornwall in 1927 and came to the notice of Stanhope Forbes . . . Painted a great deal in the environs of Falmouth but also in Brittany, the Loire valley, and the Greek islands . . . Although early in his career he was regarded as a protégé of Forbes he was largely uninfluenced by the so-called "new realism" of the Newlyn school . . . Like Alfred Sisley, whom he greatly admired, Tate was a painter of nature, and his work, though late, was in the main stream of Impressionist tradition.

'Despite a disabling stroke in 1970 he continued painting and, surprisingly, his work acquired an increased vigour; he adopted a more varied palette and made use of more vivid colours. It has been said that in recent years his allegiance shifted from Sisley to Monet!'

'Interesting! Tate died the following year – 1977.'

Helen smiled. 'I've heard it said that retrospectives are bad for the health.'

She handed him a Lyle's Price Guide, open at the right page: 'It's three years out of date but look at the prices.'

There were three Gifford Tates recorded as auctioned during the year: 'The Swanpool at Falmouth – signed and dated 1938 . . . oil on canvas . . . £17,550; The Loire at Amboise . . . 1963 . . . £12,610; Helford Village, near Falmouth . . . 1973 . . . £21,200 . . .'

Wycliffe closed the book. 'I see what you mean.'

'But what's it got to do with your case?'

'Good question. It's an odd business and it seems to be mixed up with Edwin Garland's will. He left his art shop and studio to his niece with the exception of his tube of Winsor blue and he left his tube of Winsor blue with £1,000 to the son of Gifford Tate. Another £1,000 goes to his friend, Burger, to buy himself a pair of spectacles.'

'Sounds like Lewis Carroll.'

'Yes, the old man had a wry sense of humour though on the face of it the other provisions in his will are probably more important. The residue – a substantial chunk, was left jointly to his two offspring, Beryl and Francis. Now, with Francis dead, apparently intestate, his share goes to his illegitimate daughter, a twenty-year-old. She and her mother and, possibly, her boyfriend, are the only ones who obviously benefit from Francis Garland's death. The trouble is, I don't believe it's that simple.'

Wycliffe lazed in his chair, while Helen lost herself in the zany twilight world of Iris Murdoch. His mind drifted over the people whom he had heard about for the first time that morning, groping for some sort of perspective. He was intrigued by the trio: Gifford Tate, Edwin Garland and Papa Burger, their painting holidays and their week-ends in Burger's boat. Their expeditions recalled the all-male cultural sprees which were commonplace before the first war . . . In fact the whole case seemed somehow dated. The Garlands, and their shop with the rooms over, were out of period, relics of a time when the business and management of the town had been in the hands of a few prosperous traders. Wills were of immense significance and the contingent squabbles sometimes spilled over into acts of family treachery and even violence . . .

He tried to visualise the Garland household: Edwin, widower, intelligent, shrewd, inclined to be malicious, discreetly affluent . . . Despite his chosen role as a small-town shopkeeper he seemed to have been accepted on equal terms by talented cosmopolitans . . . He had married a beautiful wife.

His son, Francis: goggle-eyed, unprepossessing, in love only with himself and his notion of some sort of scholarly distinction. A youthful affair gave him a daughter, apparently without encumbrance. On two days a week he peddled art and printing materials around the country and, for the rest, he was nominally in charge of his father's printing works. Finally, according to the lawyer, it's likely that he was having a covert affair with a woman.

And Beryl . . . Beryl, with her tunnel vision in all matters of opinion and morality, played out her role of self-sacrificing daughter and sister to the men of the house. Beryl had a friend, and both were partial to little nips of whisky . . .

Downstairs in the shop, Cathy Carne, the niece, competent and a realist. She knew that her uncle's death would radically change her position but did she, as she said, believe that the change would be for the worse?

In all that, was there any motive for murder? Of the old man perhaps, but it was the son who had been shot.

Wycliffe shifted irritably in his chair. 'Let's go to bed.'

Helen put down her book 'A night-cap. Or would you prefer cocoa?'

CHAPTER FIVE

Next morning Wycliffe spent three hours at headquarters dealing with administrative routine: departmental reports, inter-departmental memoranda, overtime schedules, and duty rosters. Diane, his personal assistant, hovered ready to guide, caution and instruct. Then he spent half-an-hour with the Chief discussing the case. His lordship was moved to reflection.

'It looks like being another of your museum pieces, Charles. When you and I joined the force the majority of homicides were like that – family affairs, or at least concerned with intimate human relationships: legacies, jealousies, frustrated passions – always with a powerful personal element. What the papers called "human dramas". Now killings are more often than not anonymous, motiveless in the sense that there is no relational link between the killer and his victim. A man is murdered because he is a policeman, a security guard, a cashier, a black man, a white man, an Arab or a Jew. At the extreme, his death may be entirely incidental to some criminal lunatic making a political point, or just blind violence like the Belgian supermarket killings. Against that sort of background the old-style domestic homicide seems almost cosy.'

Wycliffe, anxious to get away, kept comment to a minimum.

The Chief sighed. 'It's part of the pattern, Charles; society disintegrates before our eyes and we are expected to paper over the cracks.'

It was mid-day before Wycliffe made his escape. He had his week-end bag in the car and, short of an emergency, it would be several days before he was home again. He lunched at a pub on the way down and arrived at the Incident Room shortly before two. Kersey and Lucy Lane were head to head over the reports. He felt that he had been a long time away.

Kersey said: 'We've no grounds for continuing to hold Terry Gill. I've got his statement and they're letting him go.'

Wycliffe turned to Lucy Lane. 'Anything from you? How did you get on with Anna? – and, by the way, what surname did she take?'

'Her mother's maiden name – Brooks; she's Anna Brooks. I got next to nothing from her, sir. Astonishment at her legacies – genuine, I'd say, though I couldn't be sure; she's a deep one. Intelligent. I must admit I liked her; she won't squander her grandfather's money, that's for sure. It seems she saw her father five or six times a year and her grandfather less often than that, though the old man used to send her substantial cash presents at Christmas and on her birthday.'

'And her mother?'

Lucy smiled. 'Fat, lives on junk foods, strong tea and gossip; short on conventional morality, I'd guess, but not a bad sort. The kind of woman I wouldn't mind having around if I was in trouble though she might be a bit of a trial at other times. She'd spread my business all round the neighbourhood but she'd lend a hand without grudging it.' Lucy was apologetic: 'I know it doesn't get us anywhere and it's subjective, but I can only say what impression I got.'

'Any mention of the boy?'

'They didn't know we'd picked him up and I didn't

tell them. Anna was tight lipped about him but mother said: "Terry is a good lad at heart. He'll be back." '

'Fair enough. The women in this case are suspects in their own right, especially if we take notice of that boy, though from what you say I can't see Anna's mother hauling herself up on the scaffolding behind Benson's, or making a run for it when the boy turned up.'

The timetable of Francis's movements after his father's death was still full of gaps but that was to be expected. Edwin Garland had been found dead by his niece at two o'clock on the Saturday. Francis spent Saturday afternoon 'making arrangements' with the undertaker. On Saturday evening he had worked in his room. Sunday was blank. On Monday morning he registered the death and spent some time with Shrimpton – the lawyer – his father's accountant, and the bank manager. In the afternoon he visited various people who had been on friendly terms with the dead man. He had used his car for these visits. On his return he wrote several letters rather hurriedly because he was anxious to catch the post. On Tuesday he seemed to resume his normal routine of business calls and brought in two or three orders. On Wednesday morning he called on Dr Tate and he had the funeral in the afternoon.

At two o'clock Wycliffe collected the dead man's keys from the duty officer and set out along the wharf. Approach from the rear. The wharf walk had remained closed to the public in case the lab boys wanted a second bite at the cherry. The weather was changing: blue-black clouds were building in the south-east and, as Wycliffe arrived at the back of the Garlands' shop, they obscured the sun. At the same time a wind blew briefly across the harbour, rippling the water and putting the gulls to squawking flight.

It was the first time he had taken a real look at the premises from the back. The building was of a slatey stone, pointed and well maintained; two floors and a couple of attics. The ground floor windows were low enough to look in and he could see into the little office, which was empty. The other windows must belong to the studio but the lower panes were dirty on the inside so that it was difficult to see anything. All the ground floor windows were fitted with iron bars, a sufficient deterrent for the average break-and-enter boys.

He tried the door of the side passage and, to his surprise, found it unlocked. He went right through the passage to the street and entered the shop like a customer. Cathy Carne and her assistant were both serving and he had to wait. Cathy was pale and drawn and she looked tired – not, he thought, like a woman who, expecting the sack, had found herself owning the business. When she was free she took him into the office and sank into a chair as though exhausted.

Wycliffe held out Francis's keys. 'Is the studio key amongst these?'

She examined the bunch and picked out a key. 'That's it, I think.'

A five-lever Chubb. The old man had believed in security, inside as well as out.

As he was about to leave the little office he turned back. 'Do you know if Francis had a woman friend?'

'I shouldn't think so.'

'There's Anna.'

'Proving that he's capable? I'd say it was interest he lacked.'

Evidently Francis had never made advances to his cousin.

A new thought occurred to Wycliffe. 'Tuesday was the day he went off in the van and came back with a bruised face; presumably you've got a record of the people he called on that day? Of course it's possible that he made other calls not in the line of business.'

'I wouldn't know about that but I can tell you the business calls he made.' From a drawer of her desk she brought out a number of pink slips clipped together and she separated the top three. 'These were his only calls – all deliveries promised for that day.'

Wycliffe looked the slips over. 'Do you know these people?'

'Only as customers. Bestway Arts and Crafts is a small business in Hayle, dealing mainly in craft stuff; they carry a stock of art materials as a sideline. It's run by a chap called Ferris . . . The Archway Studio is just outside St Ives and belongs to a woman painter called Eileen Rich. All I know about her is that she's twice a widow . . . Ah, I'd forgotten about this one: Kevin Brand, there could be a connection there. I've got a feeling he used to live in Falmouth. He has a place out on the downs between St Ives and Penzance, a school of occult studies, would you believe? He runs day classes and in the summer he takes residential students. We print his prospectus. It's possible that Francis found a kindred spirit there.'

Wycliffe made a note of the names. 'Now I'm going to take a look over the studio and I think you should be with me.'

'If you like.'

Having looked at the studio from the outside he was prepared for squalor, but a basic orderliness surprised him. It seemed to be a combination of workshop and studio. There were two easels, and the one near the door had a picture on it, a striking painting of the Falmouth waterfront. It was painted in blocks of flat colour, cleverly apposed, with more regard for pattern than form. Wycliffe was reminded of a stained glass window.

'Is this your uncle's work?'

She was examining a few canvases stacked against the wall but she looked up at his question. 'Yes.'

'Is this where you found him?'

She came over. 'Yes, he had a habit of propping himself on that stool in front of a picture and it must have gone over with him. When I found him his body was sprawled over the stool.'

'And this picture was on the easel then?'

'Yes.'

'Had he been working on it? It seems finished.'

'He may not have been working on it; more likely he was deciding how to frame it.'

Wycliffe looked at the painter's trolley drawn up by the easel. Tubes of colour laid out tidily; there were containers for oil and turps, and two jars containing brushes.

He glanced at the tubes. 'No Winsor blue?'

'No.' But she did not smile.

'And no palette.'

'What? He wouldn't have needed one if he wasn't painting, would he?' She went back to her stacked canvases.

'May I look?'

There were twelve or fifteen finished pictures, all painted in the same manner as the one on the easel, patterns of glowing colour, but the subjects ranged from harbour and river scenes to landscapes with figures.

'So this was your uncle's style?'

'Yes. It was the style he seemed to prefer though he didn't always stick to it. He was attracted to Gauguin and the Pont Aven group.'

'In contrast with Gifford Tate.'

'Yes, Tate saw himself as an Impressionist.'

'And Burger?'

'Burger wasn't in the same class as the other two, he didn't pretend to be.'

'But he must have been keen.'

'Yes, he's very knowledgeable about painting and painters but not much of a painter himself.'

Her answers were terse, her manner preoccupied, and she was restless. She moved to another part of the studio and started to turn over a number of stretched canvases, all of them blank.

'What are you looking for?'

'I'm not looking for anything.' She realised that more was called for and went on: 'I'm curious because I've never had a chance to look round here before.'

'Not when your uncle was alive?'

'No, he kept the studio locked except when he was working, then he hated to be disturbed.'

Dark clouds now covered the sky and what could be seen of the harbour was a study in greys, slate blues and silver. It was starting to rain, fat drops slid viscously down the window panes. Cathy switched on the studio lights, further exposing its tattiness but adding to its intimacy.

Wycliffe had found Edwin's books stacked on two tiers of rough shelving. All of them were the worse (or better) for much use. No glossy volumes of coloured reproductions; most were concerned with the history and philosophy of art – Tolstoy's *What is Art?* Collingwood, Roger Fry, Greenberg, Arason, Rewald . . . not forgetting Fischer with the Gospel according to the Comrades. There were studio manuals – one with a flyleaf inscription: 'To Eddie from Gifford. Christmas 1936' – and five or six sketchbooks with pencil and watercolour sketches. If, in his paintings, Garland had sacrificed form to colour and design, it was not because he couldn't draw.

Cathy was continuing her inspection as though she would make an inventory.

Wycliffe said: 'It's all yours now.'

'Yes, I suppose so.'

'Is it possible that there was some secret in your uncle's life which he confided to Francis and which Francis tried to use to his advantage?'

He wondered why portmanteau questions always turned out so damned pompous.

Cathy Carne was derisive: 'You mean did uncle have a secret, which Francis could use to blackmail somebody else? A bit unlikely, wouldn't you say? In any case if he had a secret, Francis is the last person he would have told.'

'Yet we have evidence that your uncle did tell Francis something about himself which Francis found it hard to believe.'

She became obstinate. 'In that case I've no idea what it could be. It all sounds very improbable.'

He was moving about the studio with an apparent aimlessness looking at whatever caught his eye. He examined the rack of mouldings used for making frames and seemed interested in the machine for mitreing the angles. There was a small knee-hole desk and he went through the drawers but found nothing more than discarded pens, broken pencils, old catalogues, a quantity of scrap paper, and an assortment of pins and clips.

From time to time Cathy Carne looked across at him with obvious unease. No doubt she was wondering what it was he expected to find. He wondered himself. What was he doing, prowling about the old man's studio like a nosey neighbour? Either the place was worth searching or it wasn't. Turn it over to a couple of men to take the place apart, or leave it alone. 'You lack a professional attitude, my boy!' He'd been told that often enough in the old days. Time to behave like a policeman.

'We have a witness to the killing.'

She turned abruptly. 'A witness? You mean somebody saw Francis killed?' Unbelieving.

'From a distance, yes. The witness is under the strong impression that Francis was attacked by a woman.'

'A woman? . . .' She seemed about to add something but did not.

'Where were you on Wednesday night?'

She made an angry movement but controlled herself. 'I suppose you have to ask that. I was at home all the evening.'

'Alone?'

A momentary hesitation, then: 'Yes.'

'It would be sensible to tell me the truth.'

'I've told you. I was alone.' She turned away.

'Your flat is within two hundred yards of the spot where Francis was killed. You can see the place from at least one of your windows.'

'I've told you; I knew nothing about what had happened until I was at work next morning and one of your policemen came with the news.'

'What did your uncle say in his letter to you?'

'I've told you.'

'No. Your answer was an evasion.'

'I told you that the letter gave me advice on how to deal with the family and that is all.'

'I'll leave it at that for the moment but I may have to ask you that question again. Anyway, I've finished here for the present.'

'Do I get the key of the studio now?'

'Not yet.'

Wycliffe opened the door, waited for her to switch out the lights and pass through, then he locked the door and pocketed the keys. Cathy went into the shop and Wycliffe let himself out into the little hall from which stairs led up to the flat. He happened to glance up and saw Beryl on the landing. She beckoned to him mysteriously and he went up to her.

She spoke in a low voice: 'I heard you down there with her.' It was an accusation but delivered without punch. She seemed subdued, almost amiable. 'I want to talk to you. In here . . .'

She took him into the living-room and made him sit in the black leather armchair. He thought she might be on the point of offering him a nip of whisky but she did not go that far. She remained standing, evidently not very sure how to begin.

Outside a massive pall of cloud hung low over the harbour.

At last she began: 'I've come to see things differently since I've had time to think over what was in the will. I didn't understand at first. When they were lowering my father's coffin into his grave I thought to myself "It's all over!" I should have known better; he'd worked it all out, planned it move by move, just like when he was playing chess.'

'What had he planned?'

'How he could cause the maximum unpleasantness to those he left behind – mainly to me. Nobody, of course, will believe it: "He was such a *nice* man – a bit sarcastic at times but only in a playful sort of way." That's what people said about him. Even my friend, Celia Bond, says I'm imagining things, that I'm suffering from delayed shock or some such nonsense. We had words about it and I told her to go! Of course Celia was an only child – and spoilt; she can't believe that a father would get pleasure by humiliating his children. She's no idea!'

It was astonishing. Beryl was perfectly composed; she was no longer flushed and her hair was tidy; she even had a small smile on her lips. She had found an explanation of events which satisfied her, an explanation which in a curious way brought her contentment. She was being persecuted and it was part of a carefully laid plan. She was no longer the victim of chance, of a malign fate. Someone had hated her enough to . . . She could live with that, and fight back.

Suddenly the rain came, bursting out of the sky, beating against the window panes, and lashing the surface of the harbour into misty spray.

'Why should your father want to humiliate you?'

'He's done it all my life, it's nothing new. I was not the daughter he wanted. A girl child should be soft and pretty and loving; she should learn to titillate and flatter her father . . . Of course I failed on all counts and so I was ignored most of the time – passed over. "Beryl!" . . . I can hear him saying it now as only he could, turning my name into an insult.'

'Did Francis suffer too?'

'It wasn't the same. Francis was a boy.'

'How does your father continue to humiliate you now that he is dead?'

She looked at him. 'You ask that after hearing the details of his will? I'm turned out of the house where I was born whether I want to go or no, the house and the business are handed over to . . . to that woman, and I have to share what is left in a *joint* legacy with Francis!'

She broke off as though to allow this to sink in then went on: 'Father knew perfectly well that my brother and I didn't agree, that we would part as soon as possible, so he made sure that we would be tied together in all the wrangling that would go on because of the joint legacy.' She made a vigorous gesture. 'It was his idea of a good joke!'

The lawyer had said of the will: 'A recipe for in-fighting . . . I think he saw himself sitting up there, watching the fun.'

Wycliffe said, quietly: 'There will be no wrangling with Francis now.'

She took him up at once. 'No! I shall have to deal with that girl, but now I understand . . .'

'You can't blame that on your father.'

She looked at him oddly. 'You think not? Who killed Francis and *why* was he killed? I know what I said. That was when I wanted to keep whatever scandal there was, in the family. Now things have changed. When you find out why Francis was killed you'll also find that my father had a hand in it.'

She lowered her voice: 'There are still secrets. Francis knew something – he was smug enough about it. Cathy Carne had a letter handed to her by the lawyer. They are things we know about; God knows what else there is!'

'Are you saying that you feel threatened?'

She pursed her lips. 'I can take care of myself. But I shan't let him continue to ruin my life. That's what he wanted but he won't get away with it. Now that I understand I shall come to terms. You'll see! I'm not the fool he took me for!'

'Just one question: if you had inherited the shop and premises would you have kept it going?'

'Yes, there have been Garlands running that business for nearly ninety years, but it would have been run my way.'

'With or without Cathy Carne?'

A wrinkling of the nose. 'That would have been up to her.'

'But I understood that you intended to live with your friend after your father died.'

'That was because I assumed that the business would go to Francis and then I would have had no say in it.'

Back in the street the rain had eased but there was more to come. On his way back to the Incident Room Wycliffe had to weave a way through milling crowds who had deserted the beaches and taken to window shopping.

He was intrigued by the three old men: Edwin Garland, Gifford Tate and Papa Burger. A friendship, begun in their twenties, had been sustained throughout their lives. Week-ends and holidays were spent together, presumably to the neglect of their families; they had their private jokes, their shared experiences, and above all their obsession with art.

It sounded harmless, even pleasant. Did he have any reason to link their activities with the murder of Garland's son? To begin with, only the coincidence of the deaths of father and son within four days of each other; beyond that his notion of a connection had been no more than a hunch, and he had been in the business too long to back his hunches far ahead of evidence. But now, here was Beryl vigorously maintaining that her father had 'worked it all out – planned it move by move'. She was even ready to see her father's hand in the murder of his son. On the face of it, an absurdity, but was there an element of sense in what she had said?

The lawyer, the printing works foreman, and Beryl had each of them offered facets of the old man's character which suggested not only a cynical vein of humour and a streak of malice but a disdainful attitude to at least some of those closest to him.

There was a strong case for finding out more about Edwin and there were two sources so far untapped: Papa Burger and Edwin's brother Thomas.

The lights were on in the Incident Room. Another rain squall blotted out the harbour and water cascaded down the window panes. Now and then lightning flickered through the gloom, the lights dimmed, and thunder rattled every loose panel and plank in the building. Lucy Lane was typing a report.

'I've just come back from the Thomas Garlands' place, sir.'

'Let's hear it.'

'A modest house with a small garden where the grass looks as though it has been cut with nail-scissors and weeded with a forceps; a dolls' house, with nothing out of place, everything polished and dusted.'

Lucy Lane always set the scene and he liked that.

'We talked in the living-room which merges into a conservatory choked with potted plants like a burgeoning rain forest. Thomas is five or six years younger than his brother, knocking seventy; he's tall, lean and a bit owlish. He's not very talkative except on the subject of his plants. He used to teach English in a comprehensive school and he probably had a rough time of it.

'I was daft enough to say his plants looked healthy and I got the Ancient Mariner treatment; a squirt-by-puff account of how he managed it. Luckily, after a while, I noticed a framed photograph of a young man on the sideboard and diverted the flow by asking if it was of his son—'

She broke off as a blue lightning flash coincided with an ear-shattering thunder clap and released a fresh torrent of rain. For a moment or two they watched the rain bouncing off the waters of the harbour.

'It was a photograph of Mark and I heard how he'd qualified as a chiropractor and set up in Falmouth where it's uphill work. Then we got round to Edwin's death and Francis's murder. He seemed genuinely distressed but quite useless. He said his lawyer had persuaded him to contest his father's will and that he'd regretted it ever since. He would have liked to have gone to his brother's funeral but he thought it would only have made matters worse. As to Francis, well, it was inconceivable that such a thing could happen. Let's hope his son can be more helpful.'

'You haven't seen him?'

'No, I spoke to him on the phone. I thought it better to tackle him outside of business hours. I told him I would call at the house this evening but he said he'd prefer to come here. He's coming when he finishes work at about six.'

Wycliffe turned up the reports of telephone enquiries made among Francis's customers to find Kevin Brand of The School of Occult Studies, Carn Fellow, near Penzance. Brand had said, 'Mr Garland came here early on Tuesday afternoon; he delivered some printing work I had ordered and we had a brief conversation. He told me that his father had died over the weekend . . . Yes, I knew him when I lived in Falmouth five or six years ago . . .'

Worth following up.

Kersey came in and Wycliffe put him in the picture.

'You want me to see this guy, sir?'

'Find out what you can about him first. The local nicks at Penzance and St Ives must have some idea what goes on in a set-up like that on their doorsteps.' He turned to Lucy Lane: 'I'm leaving Mark Garland to you. For the next hour or thereabouts I shall be at the Burgers' house in Wood Lane.'

'They called me Papa because I was the eldest, three years older than Gifford, six years older than Eddie.' Then, wryly: 'There may have been another reason; even as a young man I was a staid sort of chap and they were a bit wild at times. I suppose I was inclined to lay down the law.' The old man laughed. 'I first met Eddie Garland at Lamorna, in 1931, I think it was, when we were both in an outdoor painting group with Birch. I've never been more than a dabbler but I've always had an eye for a painter and I saw at once that he was one. It turned out that we both lived in Falmouth. I was already friendly with Tate, and Eddie knew him through the shop, so we soon made a threesome and we kept together for nearly fifty years.'

Burger was very thin and very tall; he sat back in his armchair, his bony frame draped rather than clothed by a grey light-weight suit. He had kept a sufficiency of silvery hair, his aristocratic face was deeply lined and his yellowed teeth projected slightly under a clipped moustache. His voice was high pitched and from time to time he emphasised his points by restrained movements of his hands. Near his chair was a walking frame.

'My legs have let me down.'

But despite his disability his eyes had a twinkle and Wycliffe felt that he was in the presence of a truly contented man.

Wycliffe said: 'In 1931, as I work it out, Garland would have been twenty-one and already a husband and father.'

A wary look. 'Yes, that is so.'

'I've seen Gifford Tate's portrait of Garland's wife; she must have been a very lovely girl.'

'Oh, she was. Judy was beautiful.'

Mrs Burger, a little dumpling of a woman in linen trousers and a smock, like a Chinese peasant, was listening and smiling. 'Oh, don't be so stodgy, Martin! Mr Wycliffe will hear it all from someone else if you don't tell him.'

Burger deftly arranged the creases in his trousers. 'Ah! I have my brief! Well, Judy was an assistant in the shop and the two young people, both about nineteen, were drawn together. Judy became pregnant and, against his father's wishes, Edwin married her. The child, Beryl, was born and everybody seemed content except that gossip insisted the child was not Edwin's.'

Mrs Burger interrupted: 'With good reason! The girl had been seeing a lot of another young man, an estate agent called Jose, and that association continued after the marriage – long after! Long enough to explain Francis also.'

Burger spead his hands. 'My dear Penny, you have no reason to suggest any such thing—'

'Anyone who knew Jose and looks at Francis doesn't need a reason.'

Wycliffe said: 'Doesn't this imply either remarkable tolerance or remarkable ignorance on Garland's part?'

Burger did a tactical throat clearing but his wife had no qualms. 'Of course it does! But nobody has ever been able to decide which. I doubt if anyone ever dared broach the subject to Edwin and sometimes I think he simply believed what he wanted to believe, that the two were his.'

'Because he was so deeply in love with his wife?'

Burger sighed. 'My goodness, we are getting into deep water!' He glanced up at the mantel clock, then across at Mrs Burger. 'Do you think, perhaps, a cup of tea, dear? It's about our usual time.'

Mrs Burger left them alone and Burger looked at Wycliffe with a small self-conscious smile.

It was raining hard now, beating on the window panes, and the room was in semi-darkness. A pleasantly neutral room: dove grey walls, a Persian square on the floor, grey velvet curtains and white woodwork. But on the walls Edwin Garland's pictures glowed with dramatic intensity and a curious effect of translucence.

'You obviously admire Garland's painting.'

'Oh, I do! I think Garland was a truly notable painter, and very versatile. He chose to paint in this particular style but his earlier work was quite different.'

Wycliffe teased. 'All this despite your legacy?'

A dry chuckle. 'Edwin was always a joker but the point was that he seemed to undervalue his own work and to think less of my judgement because I did not. I often told him – and so did Tate – that he did himself less than justice by being content to stand in Tate's shadow. Gifford painted excellent pictures, very pleasant pictures – he was a painter of nature, but that, in my opinion, is not of itself art; I agree with Gauguin's cautionary advice to a young novice: "Don't copy nature too much. Art is an abstraction."'

'You have none of Tate's pictures?'

'Oh, yes. I have two, but not in this room. The works of the two painters don't make good stable mates. In any case my Tates are on loan to the exhibition – you know about the exhibition, I suppose?'

'Yes, indeed.'

'A big thing; Edwin was largely responsible for getting it off the ground. He put me on the committee and now they've persuaded me to open the thing.'

'Garland seems to have been a very modest man.'

Burger put the tips of his fingers together and

considered what he would say. 'Modest? Modest in the sense that he never proclaimed his talents – and they were real and varied: he was, I have heard, a very good businessman, and I know him to have been a first rate chess player and a notable painter.' Burger shifted his position and looked at Wycliffe with a gentle smile. 'But people who know their true worth often do not feel the need to go about asserting it. I do not think that Edwin set any great value on other people's opinions.'

'What do you know about Winsor blue? I understand that it was the subject of another of Garland's jokes?'

The old man nodded. 'Yes, it was, but it was something between Gifford and Edwin. I was never in on the joke, whatever it was. All I can tell you is that Winsor blue is one of the trade names for an intense blue pigment, copper phthalocyanine, which came into the palette sometime in the thirties. It was favoured by many painters as a substitute for prussian blue. Gifford dated his success from the time he started to use it; he signed his pictures with Winsor blue and a dab of the pure colour occurs somewhere in them, a sort of trademark.' Burger spread his hands. 'Painters are as superstitious as fishermen. By the same token, Edwin told me that Gifford stopped using it after his stroke.'

From somewhere in the house came the rattle of teacups on a tray. Burger leaned forward quickly and, lowering his voice, said: 'Returning to our earlier subject, Garland half believed himself to be impotent – he probably was, but he was obsessed by that damned girl he married and although she was good to look at, that was all – she was an immoral woman! Ah! That looks very nice, my dear! . . . Could you place that little table, Mr Wycliffe? . . . These legs of mine!'

'Lemon or milk, Mr Wycliffe?'

They drank a highly aromatic China tea and ate little

biscuits made with rice flour and honey, spiced with cinnamon.

Wycliffe said: 'Gifford Tate's pictures are fetching high prices. I thought any well-known painter's work tended to slump in market value for several years after his death.'

Burger sipped his tea and patted his moustache. 'Yes, but that isn't a law of nature, Mr Wycliffe; it is sometimes the result of manipulation. It gives interested parties a chance to buy in cheaply. Then, in a few years, one or two judiciously placed magazine articles, the odd programme on TV, an opportune book, and the painter is resurrected with all his best work in the right hands.'

'But Tate's pictures seem to have avoided the doldrums; his prices have much more than kept pace with inflation.'

'Because Edwin, as Gifford's art executor, was very astute and Marcella has much to thank him for. Gifford left most of his money, and the income from his pictures, to Marcella while the house went to Alan.'

'Let me see; Alan is Tate's son – the doctor.'

'Yes, the doctor – a very good one, too. Alan has compassion and that's all too rare in his profession.'

'And Marcella?'

'Marcella is Gifford Tate's wife.'

Mrs Burger amended: 'She is Gifford's *second* wife. His first left him while Alan was still at school. Gifford was sixty-one when he married Marcella, then twenty-two. So she is about the same age as her stepson. People who don't know them take them for man and wife.'

Burger smiled: 'But there will be very few who do not know if it is left to you, dear. Anyway! Tate left a number of finished canvases which had never been shown and Edwin decided to release them at the rate of one a year through Ismay Gorton's, the London gallery which handles his work. It has become a minor occasion in the art world. Each year since Tate died the "new Tate" has been unveiled with champagne and gourmet titbits for those privileged to receive tickets for the preview. I attended the first two or three, before my legs started to trouble me.'

'And these unveilings have been going on for eight years? Are there more to come?'

Burger held up a thin hand. 'I'm not sure, but Edwin told me once that there was less than a dozen pictures altogether. Meanwhile, of course, there is this touring exhibition. Will you be going to see it, by the way?'

'I shall try to.'

Burger looked at him with an odd expression. 'I think you should come to a personal preview on Sunday afternoon when I shall be there making sure everything is ready for Monday.'

Wycliffe drove back to the Incident Room with rain lashing against his windscreen. From the fading elegance of tree-lined Wood Lane to the Wharf car park is no more than 500 yards for a purposeful crow, but for a motorist on the one-way system it is the better part of a mile.

So Edwin Garland had almost certainly been incapable of fathering a child. If that was the discovery Francis had made and mentioned in his diary it might have caused him distress but it was hard to see it as providing a motive for his murder.

From his visit to the Burgers, Wycliffe had learned something about art, more about the art trade, and a good deal about Edwin Garland, but he wondered whether it had brought him any closer to establishing a motive for the murder of Francis.

Kersey, kite flying, with a wary eye on Wycliffe, expressed the same doubt. 'This guy was shot at night, on a deserted bit of the wharf. I'm not saying it was a mugging, muggers don't use guns, not on our patch they don't – yet. The chances are we shall turn up some perfectly simple motive. I don't see why we have to drag in father and father's pals with all this art business. Of course I'm only an ignorant peasant and I don't understand these things.'

Lucy Lane rose to the bait and, if she felt out-ranked, she didn't show it.

'I don't see where that argument leads. Garland was murdered because he was Garland, or it was a motiveless killing, or it was a mistake. The fact remains that he was murdered on the night after his father's funeral and if the two are unconnected we are back in the funny coincidences department. That's why father comes into the picture, art or no art.'

Kersey grinned. 'There now, see what it is to have the logic! All I'm saying is that we don't have to go groping about in corners looking for motive, there's plenty of it lying about. His daughter Anna might well have expected to benefit from his death. Her boyfriend likewise, though indirectly. Then there's Cathy Carne. According to her she was convinced that Francis would inherit and dispose of the business, but she might have thought she could do a deal with Beryl. In fact it's not impossible they had an arrangement. Although I can't see Beryl clambering over scaffolding with a .32 tucked in her pants, she'd be quite capable of doing it by proxy. Until she knew what was in the old man's will she and Cathy seem to have been matey enough. Last, but not least, there's the shadowy woman referred to in his diary.'

Wycliffe said: 'Coming down to earth, have you found out anything about Brand?'

'Nothing about the local connection yet but I've had a word with the boys at Penzance. Seems he bought a small-holding on the moor a few years back and set up these classes. I gather there are plenty of crackpots who go in for that sort of thing. It's probably harmless, even pleasantly nutty, and Brand makes a living out of them but there's another side to his business: the school attracts more than its share of gays, especially for the residential courses in the summer.'

'You're looking into the local angle?'

'Curnow's handling that, sir.'

Less than 36 hours after the discovery of the body, facts were coming in at a fair rate, though it was still not possible to decide which were relevant and which not. DS Shaw's computer, over in the corner, blank-faced and brooding, was being well fed on a mixed diet.

CHAPTER SIX

Wycliffe was booked in at a hotel on the waterfront, up river from the wharf and facing the village of Flushing across a narrow stretch of water. For a century or more, in the age of sail, the hotel had been associated with the Packet Service, when Falmouth was the port through which overseas mail and important travellers entered and left the country. Now, with its near neighbour the yacht club, it caters for nautical types of the amateur sort who enjoy messing about in boats. Appropriately the dining room seems to rise almost directly out of the water.

Wycliffe shared a table with a merchant captain whose ship was in dock, a quiet spoken man on the verge of retirement. He had a cottage in the Cotswolds waiting for him and his wife to move in.

'What will you do – in retirement, I mean?'

The Captain laughed. 'Grow roses and keep hens – isn't that the recipe for retired seamen? No; I shall be satisfied just to stop worrying about schedules, cargoes, bunkering, crews, port dues and God knows what else. I'll get by.'

They ate chicken with tarragon, followed by fresh peaches with cream, and split a bottle of Chablis between them.

The case, reported in local newspapers and on the radio, was being talked about, and Wycliffe was aware of other diners watching him. Perhaps generations of detective story writers, from Wilkie Collins down, are responsible for the romantic image of criminal investigation, so that even for a modern hard-bitten public the initials C.I.D. retain a certain mystique.

'You're a celebrity,' the Captain said.

During the meal the rain stopped and the clouds cleared magically, giving way to one of those serenely peaceful summer evenings when harbour and estuary seem embalmed in golden light and one feels that the whole world is waiting.

Wycliffe decided on a walk and his walk took him along Green Bank and down the High Street, where crumbling houses and shops were being rejuvenated or demolished, into the main street.

The Captain had set him thinking about retirement. What would he do when his turn came? Living in a cottage in the Cotswolds or anywhere else isn't an occupation. In any case he was already living where he intended to retire. 'Prepare in advance, cultivate an interest – find a hobby,' the pundits said. Well, he had plenty of interests but none sufficiently systematic to qualify as a hobby. He was not a collector; he did not watch birds, badgers or insects; photography bored him; he was not very good with his hands and the do-it-yourself world of planers, drills, jig-saws, band-saws and sanders had no appeal; he enjoyed gardens, but gardening was a chore. Perhaps he would end up like Emperor Francis of Austria – making toffee.

As though his feet were programmed he found himself at the Incident Room. DC Dixon put out his cigarette and tried to look busy.

'Just one report, sir. A Mrs Richards of Clarence Villa, almost opposite where the Tates live, says she saw Francis Garland on Wednesday morning. He drove up, got out of his car and went in—'

'We know that.'

'Yes, sir, it's in the reports, but she said he was carrying a fairly large flat package – like a picture. She didn't attach any importance to it at the time and it was only when she heard we were interested in anyone who had seen Garland between Saturday and Wednesday that she thought it worth mentioning.'

If nothing else it was a cue for a visit to the Tates.

Wycliffe said: 'You come from this part of the world, don't you?'

'I was born here, sir; my parents and married sisters still live here.'

'Do you know anything about Dr Tate? I mean, is he a popular doctor?'

'Very! It's difficult to get on his list. My mother and sisters swear by him. The funny thing is, he's not very chatty or friendly; people say he's a very shy man.'

'Any gossip?'

'Only that he's living with his stepmother who's younger than he is. People talk but there's probably nothing in it.'

Lucy Lane was at her table, typing serenely: straight back, elbows to sides, using the ten digits God had given her. The only member of the squad who could; the others hammered or pecked with two fingers, swore picturesquely, and reached for the erasing fluid. Wycliffe remembered Mark Garland.

'How did you get on?'

She swivelled on her chair to face him. 'I don't think I did, sir. He's a different proposition from his father. I got the impression that chiropractice – which turns out to be spinal manipulation – isn't a money spinner in this part of the world. Either for that reason or another he's got a monumental chip on his shoulder. He reminded me of the tight-lipped heroes in war films – the name and number ploy; more you will not get even if you carve strips off me. I tried to persuade him that he wasn't threatened, wasn't accused, wasn't even suspected of anything, but he wouldn't have it. He said: "If you think I killed my cousin it is up to you to prove it. I've no alibi. I was out running on Wednesday night at ten o'clock; I am most nights at that time." '

'You say he was out running?'

'He's a keep-fit buff.'

Wycliffe sighed.

'I asked him about his attitude to his cousin and he said he didn't have an attitude but that he was very upset.' Lucy swept her hair away from her face with both hands. 'He was certainly upset about something. I know it sounds thin, sir, but I spent a long time getting no further than that and I don't think we shall do better until we have an angle – some sort of leverage.'

'Not to worry. Something will turn up. Meanwhile we shall keep an eye on him. I'm on my way to talk to Dr Tate.'

'Do you want me with you, sir?'

Wycliffe hesitated but decided not. He located Tate's house on the wall map. It was at the southern end of 'the terraces' one of the older residential areas of the town, and not far from the Burgers'.

He had the choice of half-a-dozen alleys which led off the main street and climbed to the terraces. The alleys were steep and there were steps at intervals but there was a sense of achievement in reaching the top. His choice had more than its share of steps and when he eventually arrived on a pleasant terrace overlooking the harbour, a pounding in his chest reminded him once more that he was middle-aged. But the Tates' house was only a couple of hundred yards away.

Tregarthen – the house in a garden, Wycliffe's

Cornish stretched that far – stood, aloof from the terraced houses, surrounded by a stone wall topped by shrubs. Three or four pine trees created a sombre atmosphere in the evening sun. There were green-painted double gates and a wicket for pedestrians. A brass plate on the wicket: Dr Alan Tate MB, B.Ch., FRCP. A fellowship! What was he doing, slumming it as a GP? Wycliffe passed through into a large, well kept garden – too well kept for his taste: shrubs pruned, grass like a bowling green, edges trimmed. Why not do the whole thing in plastic? The gravelled drive split into two; one branch led to the front door, the other to the back of the house and, according to a finger post, to waiting room and surgery.

A newish Volvo was parked near the house, the off-side front had been damaged and the lamp-housing smashed.

The house itself was 1914 or a bit earlier, steeply pitched slate roofs and high chimneys: bijou Lutyens for the leaner purse. Wycliffe pressed a bell push in a door with stained glass panels. A dog yapped frantically somewhere inside and was subdued. A woman's voice, strident. Footsteps, then the door opened: a man, fortyish, glasses, slim, dark, meticulously groomed: tailored slacks, a silk shirt open at the neck and patent leather house shoes.

'Yes?' Distant.

'Dr Tate?' Wycliffe introduced himself.

Attention focused: 'Ah, yes, I suppose you've come about Garland. You'd better come in.'

A tiled hall with a large oak chest and a long-case clock. Hesitation about which room would be appropriate, then a decision. 'I've been working in my surgery, perhaps we could talk there.'

Tate spoke slowly and precisely as though each word

111

was carefully selected, examined and polished before being released.

Wycliffe followed him down a carpeted passage to a door at the end, a small room overlooking a regimented back garden with a substantial Swiss-type chalet in the middle of the lawn. Gifford Tate's studio? The surgery was equipped with the usual furniture but out of the best catalogue: desk and swivel chair for the doctor, a couple of hygienic-looking chairs for patient and friend, drugs and instrument cabinet, couch, wash basin, and glass-fronted bookcase. Parquet flooring. No dust, no smears on the polished woodwork; a faint and rather pleasing odour of antiseptic.

'Please sit down.'

Wycliffe was half expecting to be asked: 'What exactly is the trouble?' but Tate did not speak; he waited, apparently relaxed, his thin, pale hands resting on the desk in front of him.

'You attended Edwin Garland in his last illness and you were called in at his death. According to your certificate coronary thrombosis was the immediate cause of death.' Wycliffe could not have explained why he had adopted this abrupt, almost challenging approach; the doctor made him feel uneasy.

Tate still did not speak and Wycliffe was forced to enlarge. 'I'm not questioning your judgement but I have to ask whether in view of what followed you have had any doubts?'

'None whatever. Strictly speaking, Garland died of myocardial infarction resulting from a thrombus in a coronary artery.'

'Did his general condition lead you to expect something of the sort?'

Time to consider. Tate doled out words with seeming reluctance. 'Garland was seventy-five, he suffered from atherosclerosis and there was a history of anginal attacks. I warned him that unless he adhered strictly to the regimen I prescribed he would be at considerable risk.' The doctor brought his hands together and seemed to study them. 'But I fail to understand your interest in all this. Surely it is Francis's death you are investigating?'

Wycliffe was brusque. 'The deaths of father and son within a few days of each other raise questions to which I have to find satisfactory answers. You were a friend of the family, I believe?'

'My father and Edwin Garland were very close friends, so much so that I was brought up to regard Beryl and Francis as cousins.'

'And when you came back here after your father's death, to set up in practice, did you resume a family relationship with the Garlands?'

A brief hesitation. 'No. We remained on first-name terms, they became my patients, but I cannot say that there was any particular relationship between us.'

'You are a beneficiary under Edwin Garland's will, I believe?'

'A thousand pounds.'

'And a tube of Winsor blue.'

A slight gesture of impatience. 'A joke.'

'Not one with much meaning for you, I imagine?'

No response.

Wycliffe was getting nowhere, though Tate was answering his questions without protest and, apparently, without guile. In fact, that was part of the trouble, more often than not it is the protestations and evasions of a witness which tell most about him. But there was more to it than that: Wycliffe had not made contact, he had not found the tender spot which, when probed, yields a reflex rather than a reasoned response.

113

He wondered if a three-cornered exchange might be more enlightening.

'I had intended to talk with Mrs Tate also; I wonder if she would join us?'

A brief frown. 'I'm afraid that isn't possible. Mrs Tate is not at all well and she has gone to bed.'

'I'm sorry! A sudden indisposition?'

A pause while he considered his reply. 'She has been unwell for some time; she is liable to spells of nervous depression. In any case I think I can answer your questions without disturbing her.' He fiddled with the batch of NHS forms in front of him. For the first time he had been nudged slightly off balance.

A difficult man to know; perhaps shy, possibly arrogant. A meticulous man, with a compelling need for orderliness, distancing himself from anything which might threaten the harmonious life he was striving to create. When and how did he unwind? And with whom? It was hard to imagine him having a casual chat with anyone, let alone a more intimate relationship. Of course there was Marcella, but one can usually tell, from the way a man speaks of a woman, if there is an emotional involvement and, despite Mrs Burger, Wycliffe felt reasonably sure that Tate did not seek release in the arms of his stepmother.

He tried again: 'When Edwin Garland collapsed in his studio and you were called in, he was lying close to one of the two easels in the studio – is that correct?'

'The one nearest the door.'

'Was there a painting on that easel?'

'Yes. I feel sure there was.'

'Can you say which painting?'

'No, I had other things on my mind.'

'I have heard that Francis Garland brought a picture here on the morning of the funeral – is that correct?'

A faint smile – the first. 'Our neighbour has been talking, but it is quite true. Francis came to tell us about arrangements for the funeral and he brought with him one of my father's pictures which had been taken to the shop for framing. It was a tradition that Edwin should frame all my father's work but his death made that impossible in this instance so Francis returned the picture.'

Game and set.

But Wycliffe fought back: 'Will the picture be in the exhibition?'

Tate's brown eyes, enlarged by his spectacles, gazed intently at Wycliffe for a moment or two before he replied: 'No. Mrs Tate has a contract with the Ismay Gorton Gallery covering all works that were not exhibited before my father's death. I believe that it is to be shown there in February.'

Something prompted Wycliffe to ask: 'May I see the picture?'

Tate was clearly surprised and irritated by the request but after a moment or two of hesitation he said: 'Very well, if you wish. I'll fetch it.'

Wycliffe was left alone. Dusk was closing in, the garden had acquired a certain mystery in the twilight and the room itself was in near darkness. He wondered why Tate had not joined a group practice like most of his colleagues. Perhaps it was just another instance of a preference for his own company.

Tate returned with the picture. It was of moderate size – about two feet by three. He switched on the light before holding up the picture for Wycliffe's inspection. 'There you are! I am afraid the lighting is not ideal.' Sarcastic.

The village of Flushing, as seen from Falmouth in the early morning, with mist rising from the harbour. A good picture, Wycliffe thought, in the Impressionist style.

'Thank you. When was that painted?'

Tate put the picture down. 'I can't tell you exactly, but sometime after he had his stroke. No doubt it is in the record. I assume that it matters to your investigation?' The doctor was becoming more aggressive.

'I have no idea what matters or does not matter at this stage.'

Tate returned to his swivel chair. 'My father left his pictures to his wife; they are really not my concern. Edwin Garland was his art executor and looked after all the business arrangements.' He looked significantly at the little battery clock on his desk.

Wycliffe said: 'I won't keep you longer than necessary, but I should appreciate your opinion of Francis – the sort of man he was.'

'I am not a psychiatrist.'

'And you consider that only a psychiatrist's opinion would be of any value?'

A faint flush on the pale cheeks. 'I did not say that!'

'Francis Garland was your patient; did he often visit you professionally?'

'Very rarely. He seemed to enjoy good health.'

'I gather that he led a lonely life with few friends.'

'I believe that is so.'

'Women?'

A look of distaste. 'I'm afraid I know nothing of his sex life.'

Wycliffe got up from his chair. 'Very well, Dr Tate. I may look for another opportunity to talk to Mrs Tate.'

Concern. 'Is that absolutely necessary?'

Wycliffe did not answer. 'Good night, doctor.'

'I'll see you out.'

*** *

Wycliffe, unsettled in his mind, made a broad detour on the way back to his hotel. He walked as far as the beaches and along the deserted sea front. Wavelets swished idly over white sand and the broad plain of the sea stretched away into darkness. To his left, St Anthony lighthouse flashed at intervals, and far away to his right the sky was lit now and then by an arc of light from The Lizard. Nearer to hand Pendennis Castle, built by Henry VIII and gallantly defended by John Arundell against Cromwell's soldiers, brooded over its promontory, floodlit for the tourists.

Wycliffe began to feel at peace with himself and the world. He walked on, crossed the isthmus, and passed the entrance to the docks. There were houses with gardens on his left. He was suddenly aware of running feet behind him. He turned and saw a lithe figure in a track suit pounding the pavement towards him. The figure passed, breathing hard, and a few yards ahead turned in at one of the gates.

Mark Garland concluding his evening run.

When Wycliffe had gone, Tate returned to his surgery and to his records. He had scarcely settled to work when his stepmother came in followed by a sad-eyed little King Charles spaniel who immediately began exploring the corners of the room.

Marcella Tate was very pale and her skin was clear, almost transparent, so that fine bluish veins showed on her forehead and at the temples. She sat in the chair Wycliffe had vacated.

'Well?'

Tate said: 'I wish you wouldn't bring the dog in here, Marcella!'

She was immediately contrite: 'Sorry!' She stooped and scooped up the little dog on to her lap. 'There now,

Ricky, darling! . . . What did he want?'

'He knew that Garland had brought a painting here on Sunday morning.'

'And?'

'He wanted to see it and I showed it to him.'

'Is that all?'

'More or less. He asked me what I thought of Francis; whether I knew anything about his sex life.'

'What did you say?'

'That I didn't. What did you expect me to say?'

She was bending over the dog, rubbing her cheek against its head. 'Did he ask to see me?'

'Yes; I told him you were indisposed. He said that he might call on you at some other time.'

She straightened abruptly. 'Call on me? But why?' She was suddenly flushed and she let the dog slide from her lap to the floor. 'Why does he want to see me?'

Tate was staring at her, the lenses of his spectacles glittering in the reflected light. 'It's nothing to get excited about. The police talk to everybody in the hope that by hit and miss they might pick up something. You should have been here with me tonight.'

Her voice rose. 'I couldn't face it, Alan! You know I couldn't! If you—'

He came round to her side of the desk and stood by her chair. 'Don't excite yourself. You are working yourself up again. Go up to bed and I'll bring you a hot drink with something to make you sleep . . .'

The words were gently spoken and the woman pressed her head against his body with a deep sigh. 'I depend on you, Alan. You know that.'

'I know.' But he was not looking down at her, his gaze was remote; he seemed to be looking through the window into the darkness of the garden.

CHAPTER SEVEN

Wycliffe awoke in his hotel bedroom with a sour taste in his mouth and a leaden feeling in his head due to drinking with the Captain the night before. In a session lasting until one in the morning they had discussed Crime in Society with that lucidity which is only achieved at somewhere above the 100 mg per cent level of blood alcohol and with the comforting knowledge that one doesn't have to drive home. He squirmed as he recalled phrases he had used: 'Speaking as a policeman' . . . 'After thirty years in the Force' . . . 'When the State usurps the functions of the family' . . . and consoled himself with the thought that he never pontificated unless he was drunk. Or did he? . . .

It was seven o'clock by his travelling clock, and broad daylight. Because he had not bothered to draw the curtains there was a trembling mosaic of light on the ceiling reflected from the water outside and, by sitting up in bed, he could see out of the window across the harbour to Flushing. The view was almost identical with Gifford Tate's picture which the doctor had shown him – the picture that was to be the next 'new' Tate. The village was lit by a swathe of sunlight which cut through the morning mist. Several of the moored craft were caught in its path, others appeared only as ghostly forms.

He seemed to be up to his eyes in paintings, painters, painting materials, and even painters' jokes . . .

Incidentally, what was so funny about leaving the doctor a tube of Winsor blue? Or Burger £1,000 to buy spectacles? And had it in any case anything to do with Francis Garland being shot through the head? It was easy to be side-tracked by the more exotic elements in a case.

He got out of bed and drank two glasses of water from the tap then he put his head out of the window and sampled the morning air, tangy with the smell of salt water and seaweed. Away to his right the pier, jutting out into the harbour, hid the back of the Garlands' premises from his view, but he could see the scaffolding behind Benson's where Francis had undergone either translation or extinction.

Across the narrow stretch of water in front of him was Flushing Quay where the ferry was moored, ready for its first crossing of the day. A row of cottages backed on the water and in one of them Francis's illegitimate daughter, Anna, lived with her mother and boyfriend. He had not paid enough attention to Anna, he had not even seen the girl, and yet she was the only one to benefit obviously and directly from her father dying when he did. In a few days or weeks Francis would almost certainly have made a will and it was unlikely that Anna would have been the principal, let alone the sole beneficiary. In any case she would have had to wait, probably for many years . . .

He took a shower, shaved, and dressed in a leisurely way. The hotel was coming to life: in the next room a woman was scolding a child; there were sounds of pots and pans being shifted about in the kitchen; eventually, from down the corridor, came a rattling of cups and saucers. Early morning tea. Across the water the ferry cast off and its squat bulk made a bee-line for the pier. The mists were gone: a glorious morning, but according

120

to the forecast it would be short-lived. Rain before evening. The chambermaid brought his tea and he drank it avidly. Saturday: the third day of his inquiry. His shopping list for the day: Anna, Francis's hypothetical mistress, Marcella Tate, and Brand. He went down to breakfast and was relieved to find that the Captain had not yet come down. Kedgeree, toast and marmalade. Good coffee. It cleared his head.

He was in the main street before nine o'clock and many of the shops were not yet open; assistants were waiting in doorways for the boss to arrive with the keys. In the Incident Room DC Curnow was duty officer and Kersey, smoking his third cigarette of the morning, brooded over a stack of reports. Greetings were perfunctory, as between members of a family.

All the windows were wide open and the room was pleasantly cool. A couple of hundred yards away pleasure boats, preparing for trippers, were berthed three abreast against the pier. Small-boat owners were off at moorings indulging themselves, checking gear or tinkering with engines. The sea was bottle green and silky inshore, out of the sun, light blue and slightly rippled further out. Wycliffe sensed that feeling of child-like excitement and anticipation which seems to infect those who find themselves almost anywhere on the fringes of the sea on a fine summer morning.

Not Kersey: he was morose. 'I've never known anything like it: over two hundred interviews with people who were in the street, mostly in the pubs, at some time between nine and eleven on the night and nobody saw or heard a damn thing. Not even the usual nutters who invent something to get themselves noticed. And yesterday Dixon and Potter spent the whole bloody day chatting up shopkeepers and others about the Garlands in general and Francis in particular.

Nothing to show for it! The Garlands seem to have merged into the landscape. What gossip there is, is folklore: Edwin being cuckolded by an estate agent, that's still good for a laugh—'

'By the way, is that chap still around?' In order to say something.

'No, he was killed in the war. As I was saying: they dig up that and also Francis's moment of passion when he made himself a father – which must have been more than twenty years ago! If you have to go back that far to find dirt you're wasting your time. Of course they laugh at Beryl and her friend, they think Francis was a bit weird, and the old man had the name for being tight fisted, but there's no stick to beat a dog with in all that.'

Lucy Lane arrived: in a green frock figured in black, dark hair expertly set, a shoulder bag matching her frock; she looked as though she had just stepped out of her BMW runabout for a spot of window shopping. 'Good morning!' She signed the book, put her bag in a drawer, and sat at her table.

Kersey glanced at his watch. 'Nice of you to drop in.'

'I was here until after ten last night, sir.'

Wycliffe said to Kersey: 'No mistress for Francis yet?'

Kersey crushed out the stub of his cigarette. 'No, but we've turned up Brand's track record and that could mean something. When he lived in Falmouth, Brand was an art teacher, but he gave lectures on astrology and cast horoscopes in his spare time. That was probably how he met Francis, at any rate it seems they were buddies. Then, five or six years ago, Brand came into money and set up his place on the moor.'

'Where Francis visits on business. You think Francis was gay?'

Kersey said: 'I've been checking; there's nothing in

122

his diary to say that M was a woman but you can't get M out of Kevin Brand.'

'It could be a pet name, surely?' from Lucy Lane. 'My parents call me Bunny and shorten it to B.'

Kersey looked at her. 'Really? Shameful Secrets of the Manse Revealed.'

Wycliffe said: 'You'd better go and talk to him, but find somebody who knows the area or you'll spend the rest of the day chasing your tail on that moor.'

Wycliffe turned to the reports where the only item of interest was negative: not a single .32 pistol among the licensed hand guns in the register.

He put through a call to Dr Franks, the pathologist.

Franks was on the defensive: 'You've had the gist of my report, Charles. The typing is held up because my secretary has gone sick.'

'It's not your report I'm bothered about. I want some off-the-record background on Dr Alan Tate. He's fortyish, a local GP, but according to his plate he's got a fellowship. He runs a one-man practice and his patients think he's half-way between a saint and a witch doctor.'

'You think he's a quack?'

'No, I don't. All I want is some idea of why he tucks himself away down here in general practice running a one-man show—'

'You want dirt, Charles, so why not say so? I'll see what I can do.'

Wycliffe joined the trippers on the pier and made for the Flushing ferry. He had to wait a quarter of an hour, but six or seven minutes after that he was climbing the weedy steps to the quay on the other side. Although Falmouth was less than half-a-mile away there was a curious feeling of isolation. Apart from three other ferry passengers there was no one to be seen. The quay was stacked with empty fish boxes, there were platform scales, a yellow dog sleeping in the sun, a small battered truck which looked as though it had found its last resting place, and a notice about rabies. He walked past the war memorial and turned off the quay along a deserted street. The houses, whose front doors opened directly on the street, were a mixed bag, ranging from cottages to substantial dwellings of some distinction, originally built for Packet skippers. Anna and her mother lived in a little detached house which looked as though it had been sliced off from some larger building.

He knocked on the door and got no reply. He stood back and glimpsed a face at an upstair window so he knocked again and after a delay he heard someone coming down the stairs. The door was opened by a fair girl in a dressing gown, her eyes puffy with sleep. Wycliffe introduced himself.

'What time is it?'

'Half-past ten.'

'God! I overslept. You'd better come in.'

In the dark little passage she hesitated outside the door of the front room. 'That room is like a morgue, let's go in the kitchen.'

The kitchen was full of sunshine and faced across the water to Wycliffe's hotel and the Yacht Club.

'Like some coffee?'

'Yes please.'

'Only Nes – nothing fancy.'

'Where's your mother?'

She was filling the kettle at the sink. 'Gone across to Falmouth shopping, I expect.'

'And Terry?'

'Gone to work.'

'So he's back.'

'Oh yes, he's back.' She sounded resigned. She spooned coffee into the cups and added hot water, pushed over the milk jug and a packet of sugar. 'Help yourself . . . Here's a spoon . . . You want to talk to me?' She swept back her tousled hair with both hands.

'Yes. I am very sorry about your father.'

She said nothing for a moment, then: 'I didn't know him very well.'

'I hear you're going to inherit quite a lot of money.'

She stirred sugar into her coffee. 'So they tell me.'

'Did you expect anything like it?'

'No, I thought my grandfather would leave me something. He told me he was going to. Of course I didn't know about the other – coming from my father, I mean.'

'When did your grandfather tell you he intended to leave you money?'

'About a month ago. He came over one morning when mother was out and Terry had gone to work – just like now.'

'Tell me about it.'

She looked at him frowning, doubtful, then made up her mind. 'Okay. It was queer at first. He sat there, where you are, just looking at me, then, very abrupt, he said "Go and brush your hair!" I thought he must have gone a bit ga-ga but there was no harm so I went up to my room and did my hair a bit. When I came down he said: "That's better. Thank you, child!" and he just went on looking at me. In the end he said: "You are very like your grandmother, do you know that?" I said I'd seen her picture. Then he asked me to kiss him on the lips and we kissed. He held me for a minute or two, quite tight, kissing and stroking my hair, then we sat down again.

'He said that his heart was dicky and that he wouldn't

last much longer. He asked me a lot of questions about myself – what I wanted to do with my life, that sort of thing . . . He wanted to know if I minded being illegitimate . . .'

'And do you?'

'I never really think about it. Who cares?'

'What else did he say?'

'That I would have enough money to get started in anything I really wanted to do; that he thought I had enough guts to be a success if I put my mind to it. If I wanted to squander the money in six months or a year, I could do that too, but if I did he would haunt me.'

'Did you tell anyone what your grandfather had told you?'

'No.'

'Not your mother or Terry?'

'Nobody.'

She got up from her chair, went to a cupboard and came back with a crusty roll and a dish of butter. 'Have one?'

'No, thanks.'

Wycliffe tried to recall what his own daughter had been like at twenty, which was not so very long ago. Much less at ease with others or with herself, far less pragmatic; she had wanted to meet the world on her own terms – and still did, though her capacity for acceptance was growing. Acceptance, that was Anna's secret. For Anna the world was the world was the world, and she would come to terms with it.

'Did your grandfather say anything else?'

She bit into her buttered roll scattering crumbs, and shook her head. Only after considerable hesitation did she say: 'Not really.'

'I think he did.'

She frowned, wiping her lips. 'It was odd, a bit weird.

As he was going – he was in the passage – he turned round and said: "I don't suppose you know that your father and your Aunt Beryl were both illegitimate. It must run in the family, don't you think?" Then he just went. He didn't even say goodbye.' She looked at Wycliffe solemnly. 'Do you believe it?'

'Why would he lie to you?'

'No reason I can think of, but why tell me?'

Good question but not one Wycliffe was prepared to discuss. He changed the subject.

'You used to visit your father occasionally, I believe?'

'Yes.'

'Why?'

She looked at him quizzically. 'That's a funny question; because he was my father, I suppose. I mean, it's odd: I used to feel sometimes I wanted to talk to him to see what he was really like but I never did. Every time it would end up with him giving me some money. He thought that was what I came for and, in a way, I suppose he was right. I wish I had talked to him though.'

'When did you last see him?'

'At the funeral, the day before he was killed.'

'You know that Terry saw it happen?'

'From a distance.'

'He thought the killer was a woman.'

'I know.'

'I have to ask: was it you?'

She made no protest. 'No. Why should I have wanted to kill him? He never did me any harm.'

'Where were you that evening?'

'Home here, with mother.' Arms on the table, she was staring out of the window with unseeing eyes then, abruptly, she turned to face him. 'That is a lie! I was in the van with Terry.'

'He didn't say so.'

A faint smile. 'He was trying to keep me out of it.'

'Did you see your father attacked?'

'No, I'd left by then.'

'You'd better tell me about it.'

With apparent concentration she circled the rim of her coffee cup with the tip of her finger. 'After the funeral we went on the beach and in the evening to a disco. The van was on the Wharf car-park. It was one of those days, I was bloody minded . . . Anyway, in the disco we began to quarrel and just after nine we packed it in and went back to the van. Of course the damn thing wouldn't start and that was the last straw. I started nagging him about money, about not having a proper job and no guts to get one . . . You know how it is . . .' She looked up to judge whether this quiet middle-aged policeman was likely to know any such thing. She was quiet for a time and when she spoke again her manner was more confiding.

'It was the money grandfather promised me I was worried about. I'd have been a lot more worried if I'd known how much it was going to be . . . I mean, Terry isn't mean or greedy or anything like that but he would see it as a sort of bonanza, a jackpot . . . I wanted him to do something on his own.

'Anyway, he didn't say much but that didn't stop me, and in the end I got out and left him there.'

'Where did you go?'

She pushed the cup and saucer away from her. 'Tommy Webber who lives next door works in the bar at The Packet so I went along there and sat in the bar until closing time then Tommy gave me a lift home on the back of his bike.'

'Did you pass under the scaffolding on your way to The Packet?'

She shivered. 'Yes, I did.'

'Did you hear anything which, looking back, might have been suspicious?'

'Nothing, but I wasn't paying any attention.'

'This story of Terry's about going after your father to ask him for a loan to buy a small-holding – what do you make of that?'

She smiled. 'That's Terry. Of course, he didn't actually do it, did he?'

'Have you any idea of the time you left the car-park?'

'The church clock was striking ten as I came up into the street from Custom House Quay.'

Wycliffe said: 'I want you to put what you have told me into a statement. I would like you to come to the Incident Room on the Wharf later today.'

When Wycliffe returned to the quay the ferry was discharging passengers, a score or more from this trip, among them some obvious visitors, but mainly women returning from shopping in Falmouth. There was a fat woman in a floral dress, pink and perspiring, weighed down by shopping bags, who looked at Wycliffe intently. Remembering Lucy Lane's description, he felt sure that she must be Anna's mother.

But he was still haunted by the scene the girl had conjured up: the old man in that bright little kitchen with its ramshackle fittings and earthenware sink: holding her, kissing her lips and her hair; then sitting at the table, questioning her, promising to leave her some money, and finally, as a parting shot, telling her casually that her father and her aunt had both been illegitimate . . .

Marcella Tate sat on the very edge of her chair clutching her little dog to her thin breast. She looked from Wycliffe to Lucy Lane and back again with apprehension that was close to panic. Although her pallor and her drawn features aged her, Wycliffe had the impression of a little girl caught out in some childish fault.

They were in the big drawing-room of the Tates' house and the afternoon sun shone directly through the tall windows which were tightly shut, making the room uncomfortably warm.

Lucy Lane, trying to make contact, got up and stooped over the dog, stroking his head. 'My uncle used to breed King Charles spaniels. What's his name?' She spoke as she might have done to a nervous child.

'He's called Ricky – after my brother who was killed in a road accident when he was three.' She implanted a quick kiss on the little dog's moist nose.

'He looks in splendid condition. Have you ever thought of showing him?'

The two women talked dogs and Wycliffe listened, looking benign.

The room was as much a library as a drawing-room, with bookshelves occupying all the available wall space to within three feet of the high ceiling. As far as Wycliffe could see, the books were a rather austere collection of poetry, classical fiction, and biography. No pictures, but a small cabinet of porcelain figures. Wycliffe thought they might be Chelsea or Chelsea Derby. Helen would have known.

Only when Marcella had relaxed sufficiently to sit back in her chair and release her tight hold on the dog did he risk intervention: 'We came to talk about the Garlands.'

'The Garlands?' Did she lay stress on the plural?

'I'm told that Edwin Garland was a close friend of your late husband.'

A flicker of relief. 'Oh yes, he was; a very dear friend, he spent a lot of time here, expecially after Gifford had his stroke . . .'

No one spoke so she felt driven to continue: 'I expect you know that I was Gifford's second wife; I married him when I was only twenty-two and he was sixty-one. People said I did it for his money but that wasn't true. I admired him a great deal . . .'

'How did you meet him?' Lucy Lane, very softly.

'I went to a series of lectures on the history of art which he gave in Exeter where I was in my final year reading English. I got my degree before we married. I don't know why he picked on me; I've never been very attractive. But it wasn't sex that really mattered to either of us; he used to say that I was his insurance and consolation in old age.' Another nervous smile.

Wycliffe thought that Gifford Tate had found himself a girl wife, one who, however unconsciously, was looking for a daddy or, perhaps, a hero rather than a husband. Marcella would never grow up, but was it possible that, along with a childish naivety, she had carried forward into adult life the single-minded ruthlessness of the young?

She went on without prompting: 'Although he was a painter he was a very literary man so we had plenty in common. He was wonderful to talk to . . . He had read widely and deeply in so many subjects!' She turned to the bookcase: 'Those were his books, but after he had his stroke he couldn't read for any length of time without tiring his eyes and I used to read to him. In that last summer before he died I read him the whole of Proust . . . It was very hot that year and he liked me to sit naked on a chair in the courtyard garden while I read to him.' She glanced down at herself in disparagement. 'I wasn't like this, then.'

'You must have missed him very much.' Lucy Lane, without apparent irony.

'I did! I mean, he'd given me experiences I could never have hoped for. At first when he died I didn't know what to do with myself, I even thought . . . Anyway, when Alan suggested that he should set up in practice here it seemed a splendid idea.' Her eyes were glistening with tears.

'Did Edwin continue to visit you?'

'Oh yes. Not as often as when Gifford was alive but quite regularly.'

'When was he here last?'

She frowned, playing absently with the dog's ear. 'It must have been a week last Wednesday. He usually came on Wednesday afternoons because Alan is almost always here then.'

'Did he come to see you both?'

'Oh yes. The three of us would chat about anything and everything for a while then Alan would take him into the surgery so that they could be private.'

'You mean for a consultation about Edwin's health?'

'I suppose so; he was Alan's patient.'

'What about Francis? Was he a regular visitor?'

'Francis never came here.'

'Beryl?'

'Not Beryl either.'

'Had there been some sort of quarrel?'

'No! It was just that we had so little in common. I mean, Francis was a very different man from his father.'

'But Francis was here last Wednesday – the morning of the funeral, wasn't he?'

Her agitation was returning. 'He came to tell us about the arrangements, it wasn't very well organised

I'm afraid.' She said this with an air of finality as though the subject was closed.

'And to deliver a picture.'

'Well, yes. He did bring a picture with him: one of Gifford's that Edwin was going to frame for us.'

'The "new Tate" for next year?'

'Yes, but Alan will look after that now. I don't know what I should do without him. I don't think I could go on living.'

'Weren't the pictures left to you?'

'Yes, they were, but Edwin was Gifford's art executor and he looked after all the business. Gifford left me the pictures and some money, and he left Alan the house. I was afraid I would have to move when Alan came back but he wanted someone to keep house for him so it worked out very well.'

'Are there other pictures by your husband which have not yet been exhibited?'

'I don't think so. I'm fairly sure this was the last.'

'I suppose you will be at the exhibition opening on Monday?'

She frowned. 'I don't know. If I feel well enough.'

'When Francis came on Wednesday, how long did he stay?'

'About an hour, I think.'

'You were there the whole time?'

'No, I had some work to do in the kitchen and I left them here.'

'What did you talk about while you were with them?'

'About Edwin and about the funeral. That's what Francis came about. Why are you asking me all these questions?'

She was becoming worked up again and there was an element of aggression in her manner which might soon dissolve into tears.

Wycliffe became more formal. 'Mrs Tate, I have to ask you certain questions – questions which have already been put to others who were acquainted with Francis Garland, as were you and Doctor Tate. Was there any friction during Garland's visit here on Monday afternoon?'

'No! I've told you.'

'Where were you on Wednesday evening?'

Her voice was suddenly very low. 'I was here all the evening.'

'Alone?'

'No, with Alan.'

'Neither of you was out of the house after, say, half-past eight?'

'I told you we were in all the evening.'

She looked so pale that Wycliffe was afraid she might faint. He changed the subject: 'Was the chalet in the garden your husband's studio?'

She reacted with relief. 'Oh, yes. I've kept it just as it was and it's surprising how many people come to see it. Alan says we should charge . . . He's joking, of course.'

'I would like to see it if I may.'

She looked startled. 'You? Why?'

'Curiosity; interest. I admire your husband's work.'

She looked doubtful. 'I suppose it would be all right. You'd better come with me.' She led the way along the main corridor, past the surgery door. 'The key is in the kitchen; we can go out that way.'

She took the key from a hook by the kitchen door and they followed her out into a paved courtyard that was partly glazed over; there were lounging chairs, potted plants and climbers, and a sizeable lily-pond with a fountain. 'The sun comes round in the afternoon and Gifford used to spend a lot of time here after his

134

stroke. Alan and I sometimes sit out here on fine evenings.'

They crossed the grass to the studio, a substantial timber building in the style of a Swiss chalet, well preserved. Several steps led up to the door which she unlocked. The studio was a single large room open to the rafters. Windows high up in the north wall gave a diffused light. The furnishing was simple, functional and of excellent quality: two mahogany easels, a large adjustable work table, a painter's trolley, benches with shallow drawers, racks for canvases, shelves and cupboards. Two large leather-covered armchairs were placed near a cast-iron stove, and between them there was a low table with a chessboard, the pieces set up ready for play.

'This is just as it always was except that I usually have some of his sketch books, a few of his letters, and his work-book on display, but those things are on loan to the exhibition.'

She was more relaxed, taking pride in her role of showman. 'I feel like Miss Havisham – in *Great Expectations*, you know. Except that we don't have any cobwebs.' A nervous laugh.

'Is this were Edwin Garland and your husband spent their time?'

She smiled. 'Always; both of them smoking like chimneys. I fancy sometimes that I can still smell stale tobacco-smoke in here, the place is impregnated with it. Edwin rolled his own cigarettes, my husband was a pipe man. It did neither of them any good, especially after Gifford had his stroke, but there was nothing anyone could do about it.'

'Did you ever join them here?'

The idea struck her as odd. 'Good gracious, no! Gifford hated to be disturbed when he was in here whether he was with Edwin or alone.'

Wycliffe said: 'How did the stroke affect your husband, Mrs Tate?'

She frowned. 'Well, mentally not at all; physically he suffered partial paralysis down his left side. He was left-handed and so the disability was a severe blow but he used to say: "You don't paint with your hands, you paint with your heart and mind", and he proved that, didn't he?'

A good deal of wall space was taken up with framed photographs, each one labelled with a date and the location. Most we e photographs of Gifford Tate and his two friends, the settings varied from the garden of the house to the Loire Valley, and to places in the Mediterranean. Several had been taken on a yacht at sea. Women figured in some of the pictures. Marcella pointed to a rather lean, severe-looking woman with deep-set eyes. 'That's Naomi, Gifford's first wife; they separated when Alan was seventeen; she died not long afterwards.'

She opened one of the cupboards. 'This is where I keep a lot of the material for his biography. These are his sketchbooks.' A numbered series, uniformly bound in fawn linen. 'There are fifty-eight of them, dating from 1922 . . . And on this shelf I keep his letters – letters to him that is. I'm having difficulty in getting hold of letters he wrote *to* people but they are coming in slowly. I take photo-copies . . . I've got his diaries in my room; he kept a diary from the age of thirteen.'

Wycliffe thanked her for showing them the studio. 'Some of what you have told us will have to go into a statement which you will be asked to sign. This is normal procedure and need cause you no concern. You can come back with us now or you can call in at the Incident Room on the Wharf later today if you prefer.'

'I'll come this afternoon.'

Wycliffe saw Lucy Lane look at him in astonishment as he accepted the arrangement.

They were seen off after walking round the house to the front. Marcella clutching her dog, wary but to some extent relieved.

As they reached the street Lucy Lane said: 'You were in no hurry for her statement, sir.'

'What would be the point? She would only say what she has said already.'

'And this afternoon?'

'The difference, if any, will be that she will tell a story which has been revised and edited by Tate.'

'Still further from the truth.'

'Very likely; but in our business lies are often more interesting.'

At the Congress of Vienna they cut a semi-circle from one of the grand dining tables in the Hofburg to accommodate the King of Wurtemberg's belly. Detective Constable Potter would have benefited from a similar facility in the office, but his bulk was the subject of severe official disapproval and there was a parallel concern for his health and fitness. A recent medical board had told him to stop smoking, to cut down on beer, and to eat more healthily (the current euphemism for going on a diet), or else . . . But after three weeks of this Potter claimed to have lost nothing but his good humour.

'Message from Forensic, sir.' He handed Wycliffe a buff memorandum slip. 'And will you please ring Dr Franks, sir.' Morose; no hint of the chirpy fat man who had brewed more police tea than any three others, in the force, put together.

Wycliffe was moved to sympathise. 'I know how you

feel, Potter, but stick at it. I gave up my pipe last Christmas.' Smug.

Potter smiled a wan smile. 'And, with respect, sir, for the first month we all knew about it.'

'Really? Was it as bad as that?' Chastened, Wycliffe turned to his memo: 'Bullet and cartridge case submitted August 7th: Preliminary examination suggests that these belong to the same round and that the bullet was fired from a self-loading pistol of 7.65mm calibre (.32 auto. in Britain and US), probably the Mauser H.Sc. Further details later. Best – Haines.'

Haines was a friend in the right place, ready to cut a few corners and pass on information while it was still worth having.

'Call for you, sir – Dr Franks.'

'Wycliffe here.'

'Oh, Charles! A disappointment I'm afraid. Tate's reputation is impeccable, at least professionally. Trained at Kings, first class track record and his fellowship at twenty-nine. A year or two later he took up a consultancy somewhere in the Home Counties. All systems go, then his father died and he threw in his hand to set up as a GP in Falmouth.'

'Any idea of the reason?'

'A quirk of temperament apparently. Didn't like hospital work – couldn't stand colleagues – any colleagues; he's a loner. I suppose it could be that he just wants to crow in his own back yard. I don't know.'

'Anything else?'

'What more do you want? If you mean his private life he hardly seems to have had one. Dedicated or something I expect.'

CHAPTER EIGHT

'Brand bought this small-holding: house, outbuildings and a bit of land, way out on the moor. He's done a conversion job in ye-olde-worlde style, cart wheels in the yard, bare beams and brick floors, magic symbols all over the place. He runs day classes all the year round and study holidays for resident students in the summer. There are classes in astrology, the tarot, numerology, ritual magic and God knows what else.

'The attraction of the place is that it lies spot-on a ley line – an imaginary line linking a few hunks of granite scattered around the landscape, supposed to have been put there by our ancestors for their spiritual gigs. One of the features of the course is surveying, they tramp over the moor with a theodolite, a staff, surveying poles, and packed lunch, looking for other ley lines. They also go about with a galvanometer and a Geiger counter to measure "sources of power". There's a little white-washed room on the campus with a dirty great lump of granite in the middle. When they feel drained of spiritual energy the students go there and lie on the floor, their bare feet against the granite, to re-charge their batteries.'

'Sounds harmless.'

'I suppose so but the whole set-up is as camp as a field full of tents. Brand only advertises in the gay mags and, to judge from those present, that's where he gets his clients. "Most of my students come on personal recommendation." I'll bet they do.'

Three o'clock in the afternoon and the weathermen had got it wrong, the sun still shone and the sky was blue. Kersey reported on his visit to Brand.

'What sort of man is he?'

Kersey lit a cigarette. 'I know gays don't wear ID tags – "no distinguishing physical characteristics" the shrinks say, but you'd spot Brand as a card-carrying queen a mile off. Slight, fair, silk shirt, tight pants, and he walks as though he wants to wee-wee. He's friendly, but wary – very.'

'Where does Francis come in?'

'He attends classes every Sunday. Brand told me that they'd been friendly from way back and when I leaned on him a bit he admitted that they'd had a thing going but it had been broken off two or three years ago.'

'Why?'

Kersey looked like a lion with a tasty Christian in view. 'Our Frankie had found a new friend; guess who?'

Wycliffe growled, 'Get on with it!'

'His cousin, Mark. Mark turned up at these Sunday classes and despite family differences they soon realised that there was a communion of souls. Mark now spends Sundays and Tuesdays there. I don't know what the financial arrangements are but he has a double role, he attends the classes but he also does spinal manipulation and massage for those of Brand's clients who need it or say they do.'

'You didn't leave it there.' Wycliffe, being patient.

'No, Brand was persuaded to unburden himself. When Frankie arrived on Tuesday afternoon with his printing order, he got hold of Mark and they went off on their own. Frankie arrived back by himself about an hour later and drove off without a word to anybody.

When Mark turned up he was red-eyed and in a foul temper. "I thought they must have had a quarrel," Brand said, and I had the impression he wasn't heartbroken about it.'

'We must have a word with Mark Garland.'

'Here, at his home, or in his office?'

'I don't want to upset Thomas unnecessarily; let's see him in his office or whatever he calls it.'

'Mark Garland, Chiropractor', painted on the glass door of a small shop. Both door and window were curtained so that it was not possible to see inside. There was a bell-push with the instruction: 'Please ring and wait'. They rang and waited, and after a full minute the door was opened by a man in his thirties, fair, clean shaven, medium height, and slim. He wore a white coat, and glasses which seemed disproportionately large. Wycliffe had to revise a notion based on slender evidence that all osteopaths and chiropractors have the physique of rugby players.

'Have you an appointment?'

Wycliffe showed his warrant card.

'Oh, you'll have to wait. I have a patient with me.' His manner was nervously belligerent.

They were put into a little room, no more than a cubicle, where there were two kitchen-chairs and a table with a few magazines. The partitions were thin and they could hear Garland giving instructions to his patient to make certain movements and assume certain postures. It was soon over, the patient was shown out after making a further appointment, and they were admitted.

The consulting room was as sparsely furnished as the waiting cubicle; two chairs, a desk and a telephone, in addition to the essential couch. Wycliffe and Kersey were given the two chairs while Mark Garland perched on the edge of the couch.

A one-man show, not even a receptionist.

Garland opened with a protest. 'I told your sergeant that I know nothing of my cousin's death. I am distressed enough about it without having you people coming here, interrupting my work.'

Wycliffe was looking round the room. On the walls there was a certificate from a professional institution, an advertisement calendar, and a framed photograph of the harbour. It seemed that he had not heard Garland's little speech but his gaze came round eventually.

He said: 'Let us be clear about your position, Mr Garland. I am investigating a murder. You will be asked certain questions and your answers or failure to answer will decide whether or not you go with us to a police station for further interrogation. Now, what is it to be?'

Garland took off his spectacles and cleaned the lenses with his handkerchief. 'I'll listen to your questions before I decide.'

'No, I shall decide on the basis of your answer to one question: I want to know the circumstances in which your cousin received bruises to his face on the day before he was murdered.'

'I've told you I know nothing about Francis's death.'

Wycliffe leaned forward in his chair. 'And I've told you the options, Mr Garland. We know that you quarrelled with your cousin at Brand's place; he returned from the encounter with his face severely bruised. The following evening he was shot dead while walking his dog along the wharf here. We have reasonable grounds for detaining you on suspicion unless you can satisfy us that you had no part in the shooting.'

Garland was shaken and he was still making up his mind how to react when the doorbell rang. He looked doubtfully at Wycliffe: 'My next patient.'

Kersey said: 'Your notice tells them to ring and wait. This one has rung, now he can wait.'

'It's a woman. Shall I ask her to make another appointment.'

'That's up to you.'

Garland went to the door and they heard a brief exchange. When he came back he had decided to co-operate. 'Ask me what you want to know.' He perched on the edge of the couch once more and Wycliffe realised that he was trembling.

'Why did you attack your cousin?'

'We had a row.'

'You had a homosexual relationship?'

'That's not illegal.'

'No, it's a matter of fact.'

'All right, we had a homosexual relationship and it was understood between us that as soon as it was possible we would go away together and start afresh.' He could not keep still and his eyes reddened as though at any moment he might burst into tears.

'What would have made your plans possible?'

'It was understood that we would go when his father died and the will was settled. Then, when his father did die . . . Within three days . . .' He broke off, unable to continue.

'Take your time.'

He made an effort. 'Three days after his father died, when it seemed everything would begin to come right for us, that he would be able to leave that business and I would get out of here . . .' He looked round the bleak little room in despair. 'He chose that moment to accuse me of having someone else.' He pressed a handkerchief to his eyes, sobbed, and blew his nose.

'He was jealous?'

'Yes, it was so unreasonable! To threaten everything because of wicked gossip.'

'Gossip about you and . . . ?'

A sidelong look. 'About me and Kevin Brand. Because I gave Kevin massage – I mean, that's one of the reasons I go there.'

'So you attacked your cousin.'

'Yes, I attacked him, if that's what you like to call it! I lost my temper. If it had been a man and woman relationship you would think that was understandable but we aren't expected to have feelings; if we do they're a joke.'

Wycliffe said: 'I'm only interested in what happened at Brand's place on the Tuesday because of what followed.'

Garland shook his head. 'I didn't kill him. I couldn't!'

'So where were you on Wednesday evening?'

'I told you: I went for my usual run. I left home at half-past nine and I got back about half-past ten.'

'Where did you run?'

He made a vague gesture. 'The usual: Swanpool, across to Gyllingvase, along the seafront, around Castle Drive and home.'

'Not through the main street?'

'No.'

'Do you own a gun, Mr Garland?'

'Of course not!'

'Have you ever fired one?'

'Only a .22 sporting rifle when I was at college.'

Wycliffe said: 'I want you to come back to the Incident Room with me where you will be asked to make a full statement.'

'Am I under arrest?'

'No, you are helping us with our enquiries.'

More fodder for the computer if nothing else. A modern investigating officer secures his rear with computer print-out. And more enquiries to be made: anyone walking or driving along the following route between nine-thirty and ten-thirty last Wednesday evening . . . A man in a track suit, running . . .

'I thought it was a woman.' The only first-hand evidence they had and that depended on the observation of a not very bright young man, on a dark misty night, at a distance of a hundred yards.

Wycliffe reviewed possible candidates: among them the women, Cathy Carne, Marcella Tate, and Anna Brooks – any one of them would have been physically capable of committing the crime and sprinting away afterwards. And which of the men might have been mistaken for a woman? As the witness concerned, Terry Gill, had to be omitted (though he remained a suspect); that left Alan Tate and Mark Garland, both of whom were of medium height, slight of build and certainly capable of the agility required.

A reconstruction? Would seeing a re-run of the incident, as he had recounted it, help Terry Gill to a firmer conclusion? Wycliffe thought not. In his experience reconstructions were little more than public relations exercises.

Marcella Tate came to the Incident Room and made her statement which added nothing to the sum of their knowledge.

Wycliffe was late for his after-dinner walk, delayed by the Captain, but he was anxious to establish an element of routine. Without a pattern, some repetitive rhythm in his days, he felt lost.

He walked down the High Street and along the Wharf with the intention of retracing Francis's footsteps on the night of the murder. The time was about right but conditions were quite different: instead of misty rain the evening was clear, the air was balmy with that silky feel, and the waters of the harbour gleamed in the darkness. He passed the barred windows of Edwin's studio; the only light in the building came from an upstairs room, the living-room, where Beryl was almost certainly sitting and brooding alone.

He imagined Francis coming out, and the dog scampering ahead through the mist. Less than 200 yards away was the car park. When he reached it there was a sprinkling of cars but no decrepit old van with a CND symbol on its side. Had Francis seen and recognised the van? Had there, despite Terry Gill's denials, been an encounter? He passed the lighted windows of the Incident Room and continued on towards Benson's. The lights on the scaffolding shone, unwinking in the still air.

It was the first day the wharf walk had been re-opened to the public and the first night without a PC on guard at the scene of the crime. Saturday night; the pubs in the street would be doing good business but it was very quiet, only a faint hiss of escaping steam coming from the docks. He reached Benson's and passed under the scaffold. Old mortar, chipped from the wall, still crunched underfoot. At this point Francis must have had about 20 seconds to live, a few more steps and he would have reached the other end which, for him, was the threshold of death.

Wycliffe always forced himself to envisage every detail of a murder so that he would never become reconciled to the enormity of the crime. Murder appalled him because it took everything from the victim with no possibility of restitution, it blotted out memories of a past and hopes for a future. It was the supreme arrogance of the killer which dismayed him. He could not imagine the stunted, blinkered, and self-regarding mind that could contemplate the killing of another human being.

He stood for a moment or two at the spot where Francis's body had been found. The first stage of the scaffolding was little more than a foot above his head. The killer must have been kneeling there, pistol at the ready, and as Francis emerged he or she had fired at a range of a few inches.

He shuddered involuntarily and walked on towards the printing works.

He could see the rectangular outline of the building and, at the top, at the harbour end, a lighted window open to the night. He had not, so far, met Cathy Carne on her home ground and now was his chance. A moment or two later he was ringing her door bell.

There was a light behind the hammered glass and he could hear Cathy Carne's voice, speaking on the telephone. He could not distinguish her words but she sounded harassed and tense. The bell probably cut short her conversation for almost at once he heard the telephone replaced and she called out: 'Who is that?'

'Superintendent Wycliffe.'

She opened the door; she was wearing a dressing gown. She looked flushed and vaguely dishevelled. 'I'm sorry, but one has to be careful about opening the door at night.'

'Of course!' He apologised for disturbing her.

'It doesn't matter; come in. I was on the telephone.'

He followed her into the living-room. It was snug: a

sofa, tub chairs, television, record player, and shelves full of books on either side of the chimney breast. Over the mantelpiece an Edwin Garland landscape with figures. On a low table there was a tray with a bottle of whisky and two used glasses. She whisked the tray off the table and took it away. When she returned she felt the need to explain.

'Saturday is usually hectic in the shop and I'm ready for bed and a book by ten o'clock but tonight I felt the need of a nightcap. Do sit down!'

She sat herself on the sofa and pulled the dressing gown around her legs. She was watching him closely and she was talking too much. Something had upset her and he doubted if it was his arrival.

'I didn't ask you; would you like a drink?'

'No, thanks.'

She reached for her cigarettes and lit one. 'Now, what's all this about?' Working hard at trying to sound normal.

'How well do you know Mark Garland?'

'Mark?' She seemed surprised and perhaps relieved. 'Hardly at all. Odd you should ask, though, because he was in the shop last Thursday, wanting to talk to Beryl. It was the first time I've spoken to him in years.'

'Thursday was the day after your uncle's funeral, the day Francis's body was found.'

'Yes.' She was cautious.

'I thought there was no contact between the two sides of the family.'

'There wasn't – isn't; Beryl wouldn't see him.'

'Have you any idea why he came?'

She made a vague gesture. 'No; he seemed upset, edgy. He said he wanted to explain something to Beryl but I've no idea what. When Beryl wouldn't talk to him he went away more upset than ever.'

Wycliffe was taking in details of the room. Self-contained was the phrase that occurred to him; everything was there to hand. The same phrase described the woman who had made it. Not that Cathy Carne was a loner, she wanted – needed human contacts, but she would have them only on her own terms. They must arrive on the doorstep, like the milk.

'Presumably you have friends – outside of business?'

Her eyes narrowed against the smoke from her cigarette. 'Naturally.'

'Did Francis or Beryl ever visit you here?'

'Never.'

'Edwin?'

'No.'

'The Tates?'

She frowned. 'What is all this?'

'A simple question. If you would prefer not to answer it . . .'

'It's not that. As a matter of fact the Tates are friends; after all I've known them for years.'

'They come here?'

She crushed out her cigarette. 'Dr Tate comes here sometimes. To be honest he's a fairly regular visitor; he's a lonely man and we have things in common.'

'Something wrong with that? Why be coy about it?'

She wore a watch with an expanding gold bracelet and she fingered it, easing the bracelet away from her wrist and examining the pattern of indentations it left on her skin. 'It's silly really, but Alan is a doctor and vulnerable to gossip, he's also a very private man.'

'Perhaps Marcella wouldn't like it.'

'What are you suggesting?'

'Only that I have an impression that she depends a great deal on the doctor.'

'She does, but there's nothing . . . there's no attachment. That is malicious gossip.' On her metal.

'Was Dr Tate here the night Francis was killed?'

'What are you getting at?'

'Again, a simple question.'

She hesitated, then: 'Yes, he was here.'

'When did he come and when did he leave?'

'He came at about seven. I had invited him for a meal, and he left around midnight.'

Wycliffe stood up and went to the window, parted the curtains, and looked out. 'I can see the back of Benson's quite clearly. It's not far, is it? There was a shot and the dog barked, but you heard nothing?'

'Not to notice. Here, by the harbour, there are all sorts of sounds from the docks and the ships, one gets to ignore them.'

He stood, looking down at her. 'And neither of you left the flat between say eight and eleven?'

'Neither of us.'

'Good! Just one more thing. The letter your uncle left you; you say you destroyed it?'

'We come back to that!'

'And we shall continue to come back to it until you tell me what was in it.'

'I've already told you.'

'You've told me nothing which would have been worth Edwin Garland taking the trouble to put into a letter and leave it with his lawyer. It's a serious matter to mislead the police in a murder investigation. Take legal advice if you want to, but I intend to know what it was that your uncle confided to you.'

There was silence during which they could hear singing coming from the street. The clock on the mantelpiece chimed and struck eleven.

Wycliffe said: 'Have you thought that you may yourself be in danger?'

'In danger? Me?' Unconvincingly dismissive. 'I don't know what you mean?'

'Your uncle, for his own reasons, confided something to Francis and Francis is dead. Perhaps it is dangerous to have information and keep it to yourself.'

She looked incredulous. 'That is nonsense!'

'Think it over. I'll say good night and I apologise for disturbing you so late.'

She came with him to the door, uneasy, perhaps scared. She watched him go down the steps. He waited until she had closed the door then went back up, making as little noise as possible. The hall light was still on and he put his ear to the letter box; he could hear her voice on the telephone but could not distinguish her words.

Two women seemed anxious to provide Tate with an alibi, or to use him as an alibi for themselves.

He walked back along the wharf.

Wycliffe spent a restless night. Although his curtains were drawn, moonlight flooded his room and each time he awoke from an uneasy sleep he thought that it was morning. Waking or sleeping his mind fretted away at the case, images drifted in and out of his consciousness, words and phrases came to mind in a confusing jumble but once, in a doze, it seemed that Beryl was actually speaking to him in her clear, cracked voice. 'He worked it all out, planned it move by move . . .'

Beryl's words had impressed him at the time because they summed up his own vague feeling that what had happened and what was happening might be consequences of the old man's cynical, even malicious contrivings. Obviously Edwin had not murdered Francis but he had created a situation in which violence was more likely.

The main provisions of the will were devisive and

certain to breed strife, but they provided no motive for Francis's murder. How often had Wycliffe told himself that the only obvious beneficiary from Francis's death was his daughter? But could she have known that her father had not made a will? In any case he could not believe . . . but that was not evidential.

Aside from gain the commoner motives for murder are anger, jealousy, lust and fear. The first three, in combination, or any one of them, pointed to Mark Garland. As to fear, who would have reason to fear Francis? Surely he presented no physical threat to anyone, but it was possible that he had knowledge that was threatening. His father had confided in him and Francis himself had been surprised, not only by the nature of the confidence but also by the fact that it had been made to him. 'Something about himself . . . Incredible to think that it has been going on all these years . . . He said I could talk if I wanted to . . .'

Cathy Carne had also been told something in her damned letter.

But there were other provisions of the will, dismissed as harmless jokes, but were they? A tube of Winsor blue for Alan Tate, spectacles for Burger . . . 'which I hope may improve his judgement and help him to see the obvious.' To see the obvious – Wycliffe wished that spectacles might do that for him. What was obvious? The relative merits of Tate's and Edwin's paintings? That was Burger's explanation but the truth might not be so innocent.

A tube of Winsor blue for Alan Tate – a way of wishing him luck, Cathy Carne had said.

Wycliffe resigned himself to lying awake for the rest of the night but, in fact, he fell asleep and knew nothing more until he was awakened to broad daylight and seagulls squawking outside his window.

CHAPTER NINE

Sunday morning. Wycliffe pretended to believe that there was something special about Sunday mornings, a quality in the air which he would be able to recognise however far adrift he might be from any routine or calendar. Certainly everything moved at a slower pace: the day took longer to get going; even the hotel breakfast was later than on other days; but he was on his way to the Incident Room by nine o'clock.

A newspaper seller was setting up his stand at the entrance to the pier but otherwise the street was deserted; shop blinds were drawn and a capricious breeze chased after Saturday night's litter.

Lucy Lane was already on duty, as fresh as the morning. 'There's been a call from Mark Garland's father to the local nick. Knowing our interest they passed him on and I spoke to him. Mark didn't come home last night and he's worried. At a little after eight Mark told his father he was going out; he went, and the old man hasn't seen him since.'

'He didn't say where he was going or when he could expect him back?'

'No, but that's not unusual; the most he ever says is "Don't wait up for me", though he's rarely late home.'

'Did he take anything with him?'

'Apparently not, just the clothes he was wearing.'

'We'd better talk to Thomas.'

They walked along the wharf and at the Custom

House Quay they climbed the slope to the main street past the King's Pipe, a free-standing fireplace and a chimney where, in less sophisticated times, revenue men had burned smuggled tobacco. On their right, shops gave way to large houses and on their left, to the harbour. Unhampered by buildings the breeze decided that it was a south easterly and they could see white water off Trefusis Point, a warning to small craft not to venture outside.

A row of terraced houses as they approached the docks, then one standing alone, red brick – incongruous amid all the stone and stucco.

'This is it, sir.'

Thomas opened the front door before they could ring. 'Do come in! I'm rather worried. He's never done anything like this before. I didn't realise he wasn't in until this morning . . . He wasn't home when I went to bed but that's nothing out of the ordinary because I go to bed early. There's nothing much to stay up for.'

He led the way into the living-room. 'Mark doesn't tell me anything – he never has, so when something like this happens I don't know what to do. I telephoned the police because I wondered if there could have been an accident.'

On a tablecloth, folded over part of the dining table, there was a teapot, milk jug, and a cup and saucer. Sunlight filtered through the greenery in the conservatory making a dappled pattern on the floor. A tabby cat followed in Thomas's footsteps eyeing the visitors. On the wall among a number of framed photographs there was one of a youthful Thomas in cap and gown.

'I gather that your son went out at about eight last evening and you've no idea where?'

'No idea! he doesn't go out in the evenings, much, except for his running. He was on the telephone to somebody – I don't know who – I heard him say, "I'm rather worried, I would like to come and see you", and a little later he came in here, all dressed up, to say that he was going out.'

'Dressed up?'

'He was wearing a suit that he keeps for rather special occasions.'

'Did he take his car?'

'His car is in the garage.'

Suddenly Thomas remembered his manners and found seats for them but remained standing himself.

'Does he go out a lot?'

'Apart from his work he's usually out most of the day on Sundays and Tuesdays. He doesn't have patients those days, you see.'

'Do you know where he spends his time then?'

'I know that he attends classes with a Mr Brand who runs a sort of school for what they call occult studies.' A diffident gesture. 'Not something that appeals to me, but he has always shown an interest in that sort of thing.'

Wycliffe had to probe: 'Do you know that he was a close friend of Francis Garland?'

He had not known and at first he was unbelieving, but when his protests had died away he looked at Wycliffe with fresh concern. 'Are you telling me that Mark not coming home has something to do with his cousin?'

It was Lucy Lane who answered. 'We don't know, Mr Garland, but we do know that there was an intimate relationship between Mark and Francis which reached some sort of crisis last Tuesday. This happened at Brand's place, there was a scuffle and Francis came away with his face badly bruised.'

It was painful. The thirty-odd years which Thomas

155

had spent as a schoolteacher in a comprehensive school must have been perpetual torment. Shy, vulnerable, his blue eyes looked out on a world which seemed inexplicable and hostile.

He sat down by the table; the cat leapt on his lap and he stroked it absently. 'You are saying that Mark is a homosexual. Who told you all this?' He spoke sharply but he seemed less surprised than they might have expected.

Wycliffe said: 'Your son, in a statement he made early yesterday evening.'

'You've been questioning him?'

'He was at the Incident Room helping us with our enquiries into his cousin's death.'

'You're not saying that you suspected him of . . . of killing Francis?'

'No more than others.'

'And now?'

'We must find him first.'

'You're treating him as a fugitive! You think he's run away.'

Wycliffe said: 'We simply don't know what has happened. Did he seem upset or agitated when he came home yesterday evening?'

'He was just as usual, he never says much. I asked him why he was late for his meal and he said that he'd had an extra patient.'

'I gather that he took nothing with him; no suitcase – nothing. Are you quite sure of that?'

'I'm quite sure. By chance I saw him walking down the drive to the gate and he was carrying nothing.'

He was staring at his cup, turning it round and round with his fingers. 'My brother, my nephew, and now . . .'

'We don't know that anything has happened to your

156

son, Mr Garland. As a matter of routine I would like one of us to take a look at his room. You can be there, of course.'

Thomas hesitated then he looked at Lucy Lane: 'I would rather go up with her.'

Wycliffe waited in the living-room but they were not long gone. When they came down again Thomas had tears in his eyes. Lucy Lane said: 'The moment we have any news we'll be in touch.'

The old man stood in the doorway, holding his cat, while they walked the short distance to the gate.

Lucy Lane said: 'He's got a friend who will be coming in later. I feel very sorry for him. Sometimes the idea of being a parent scares me stiff, it's like offering yourself for vivisection.'

'You saw his room. What was it like?'

'Very ordinary; everything neat and tidy; not much of anything and nothing remarkable except a drawer full of soft porn gay magazines, and a collection of books on occult subjects. What did you expect?'

'Thomas knew about the magazines?'

'Of course. That was why he wanted me instead of you to go up with him. Do we put Mark on the telex?'

'Yes, we've got to find him, and the sooner the better; he's not just a missing man, he's a missing suspect.'

'Anything else?'

'We get Mr Kersey to have another heart to heart with Brand.'

'The telephone call – do you think he was keeping an appointment?'

'It looks like it and we have to find out who with.'

As they walked back through the street the church bells were ringing for morning service.

***

Mark Garland's description was circulated and enquiries put in hand at the railway station, and among bus drivers, taximen and hire-car firms. In their lunch-time bulletin the local radio would ask whoever spoke on the telephone to Mark Garland on Saturday evening and anyone who saw him after eight o'clock to contact the police.

Wycliffe and Kersey brooded, watching the racing yachts with their multi-coloured sails performing a lively ballet in the fresh breeze.

'Lucy Lane talked to him on Friday evening, here; I saw him with you in his consulting room yesterday and we brought him back here to make his statement. A couple of hours later, after a phone call, he walks out of his home, taking nothing with him, and disappears.'

Kersey rubbed his chin, always bristly however often he shaved. 'Do you think he's done away with himself?'

'Putting on his best suit for the occasion?'

Kersey nodded. 'That's a point. But where does it all leave us?'

'Still searching for a missing man.'

Kersey pitched the stub of his cigarette through the open window.

'Assuming his innocence, his disappearance would be convenient for whoever did shoot our Frankie.'

'The same thought occurred to me.'

At eleven o'clock there was a telephone call for Wycliffe. 'Dr Tate speaking. I've just heard that Mark Garland is missing and I think I should tell you that he was here with me yesterday evening.'

'Was he visiting you as a patient?'

'Yes, although I have no Saturday surgery—'

Wycliffe cut him short. 'It will be best that we meet and talk. I'll be at your house in a few minutes.'

'But—'

'If you please, Dr Tate, in a few minutes.'

'All right.' A grudging concession to the inevitable. 'But please come round the back to my surgery. I don't want Mrs Tate disturbed.'

Wycliffe said to Kersey: 'I want you to meet this man.'

They drove to Tregarthen, walked up the drive under the pine trees, and round the back of the house to a door marked 'Waiting Room. Please Enter'. Before they could do so the door was opened by Tate in person and they were ushered through the empty waiting room into his surgery.

'Please sit down.' The doctor was wasting no time.

Wycliffe introduced Kersey, and Tate looked at him with a certain wariness. 'I find myself in a rather invidious position . . .'

Tate was meticulously turned out, perfectly shaved, his hair had been recently trimmed, his pale hands were manicured and the cuffs of his shirt just showed below the sleeves of his jacket. On the desk in front of him was a medical records envelope labelled Mark Garland.

'As you know, Mark Garland is a chiropractor and though I do not subscribe to the principles of chiropractic I recognise the value of skilled manipulation in certain cases. Garland is a natural and I have referred a number of my patients to him with good results.'

'So you had a professional relationship with the missing man. How did you hear that he is missing? It is not public knowledge.'

Tate was not pleased at this brusque approach but he explained: 'Garland left his wallet behind, it must have slipped out of his jacket when he took it off for me to examine him. At any rate I found it on the floor this morning; I telephoned to tell him and spoke to his father. Of course he told me that his son was missing

159

and that you had already started an investigation.'

'What happened yesterday evening?'

A pause, then: 'He telephoned concerning a patient I had asked him to see and he took the opportunity to tell me that he was worried about his own health. After running the previous night he was experiencing certain symptoms which, he thought, might indicate heart disease. It sounded unlikely but he was clearly in an anxious state of mind so I suggested that he should come and see me right away.' Tate paused and sat back in his chair. 'He was here within fifteen minutes.'

The sun had not yet reached the back of the house so that the garden was in shadow and the room itself in a gloomy half light. No sound came from outside and Wycliffe felt that the world had been consciously excluded, that he and Kersey certainly, and even the patients who regularly gathered behind the padded door, were intruders. They might be inevitable, even necessary, but they were not welcome.

Tate was looking at Wycliffe as though he expected a question but when none came he continued: 'I examined him and decided that whatever his symptoms they were almost certainly mental rather than physical in origin. I told him as much and he admitted that he was under considerable stress. Among other things he said that he found difficulty in sleeping. I prescribed nitrazepam, to be taken for a few nights on going to bed, and told him to see me again in a week.'

Tate spread his hands. 'And that was all. He left here reassured, at least in regard to his physical well-being. I must say that it was a considerable shock to learn that he seems to be missing.'

Wycliffe said: 'What time did he leave?'

Tate considered. 'He was here for about forty-five minutes. He must have left at nine o'clock.'

Kersey said: 'Did he tell you what was worrying him?'

So far the doctor had spoken directly to Wycliffe, but from time to time he had cast uneasy glances in Kersey's direction. Certainly Kersey's presence seemed to disturb him but, after only a brief hesitation, he answered the question: 'Not in so many words.'

'But you have some idea of what it was?'

Tate looked at him blankly and said nothing.

Wycliffe intervened: 'I'm sure you understand, Dr Tate, that the confidentiality of the consulting room has no protection in law.'

Somewhere in the house a clock chimed and struck twelve.

Tate sat back in his chair as though making up his mind about something then he said: 'I am reluctant to discuss what a patient tells me in confidence but I suppose I have no choice. Garland was worried about being interrogated by the police in connection with his cousin's murder. He told me of the incident in which Francis got a bruised face and of what led up to it. All this, of course, you already know so I am really betraying no confidences.'

Wycliffe chose his words with care. 'You say that he was worried because we questioned him; would you say that his concern went deeper than that?'

Tate made a vigorous gesture of rejection. 'I know what you have in mind but I refuse to be drawn along that line. You are no longer asking me for facts but for speculation. All I can say is that he was deeply disturbed.'

Kersey tried another approach: 'As an experienced medical man and knowing your patient well, would you be surprised if it was found that he had taken his own life?'

161

Tate pushed away the folder containing Garland's medical records as though symbolically dissociating himself from the question. 'Really, you put me in an impossible position! If I had thought that there was any such risk when he was here last evening I would have taken precautions.'

'But on reflection?'

Tate placed the tips of his fingers together and regarded them. 'On reflection, I will say that I wish I had taken his mental condition more seriously. But that doesn't mean that I think he killed himself.' He got up from his chair. 'Now, Mr Wycliffe, if you will excuse me, I have some work I want to do before lunch.'

Wycliffe remained seated. 'I have some further questions for you, Dr Tate. Do you have any idea where Garland might have gone when he left you?'

Tate frowned. 'I assumed that he would have gone home. Where else? You must understand, Mr Wycliffe, that my only connection with him is by way of an occasional professional encounter. I know nothing of his private life. Your next question?'

'Did Mrs Tate have any contact with him while he was here?'

'Mrs Tate? Certainly not! It was not a social visit.'

Wycliffe stood up and so did Kersey. 'Thank you, Dr Tate; that is all for the moment.'

Tate was distant. 'I hope that Garland turns up safe and well, but there is nothing more that I can tell you.'

They were escorted out, not through the waiting room, but through the house and out by the front door.

As they walked down the drive they saw Marcella crossing the lawn with her dog. She walked with jerky self-conscious strides and made a point of not seeing them.

Wycliffe closed the wicket gate with a sigh. 'Claustrophobic, wasn't it? What did you make of him?'

Kersey took a deep breath. 'He didn't need much persuasion to overcome his professional scruples. I had the impression that he wanted to tell at least as much as he did tell, and at one point he seemed to be hinting that Mark might well have killed his cousin.'

They were in the car before he spoke again: 'It seems to me that when we know what happened to Mark Garland we shall be in business. Either he is a killer on the run, who may have done away with himself, or he's another victim.'

Wycliffe fastened his seat belt. 'Finding out which is our biggest problem.'

Kersey was driving. Wycliffe never took the wheel if he could avoid it. As they turned away from the terraces, downhill towards the town centre, Kersey said: 'If Mark Garland wasn't the killer then we are up against motive. Somebody killed Francis and presumably they had a reason. At any rate, he's dead.'

Back in the Incident Room Wycliffe slumped into a chair. The duty officer handed him a memo slip. 'Telephone message, sir.'

The message read: 'Expecting to see you at your personal preview this afternoon at 3.00. Burger.'

Kersey said: 'I get the impression that we are being taken for a nice smooth ride but unless something breaks I don't see what we can do about it. On Tuesday afternoon Mark Garland had a set-to with Francis who had bruises to show for it. Jealousy among gays can be every bit as vicious as among heteros and on Wednesday night Francis is deliberately murdered by someone lying in wait for him on the wharf. Mark is questioned a couple of times and fails to give a satisfactory account of himself but there is nothing on which to hold him, then he disappears. If he is never found there is a nice tidy case; no more police time wasted, no trial, no burned fingers, and public money saved. Nobody to complain but the lawyers, and who loses sleep over them?'

Wycliffe shook his head. 'Nobody is going to sweep this one under the carpet.'

'So what do we do?'

'At the moment what can we do, except the obvious? – enquiries in the neighbourhood of the Tate house: anybody who saw Garland arrive, anybody who saw him leave, and anything else they can pick up.'

At three o'clock Wycliffe arrived at the Gifford Tate exhibition. He was admitted by an earnest-looking young man with large spectacles and a lisp. Burger, athletically ambulant in a wheel chair, was cordial. A severe looking matron, with a plummy voice and tinted hair, was unpacking catalogues. A young woman was checking the labels on the pictures against the numbers and descriptions in the catalogue.

'You see! My helpers do all the work while I potter.' He picked up one of the catalogues in the glossy, illustrated edition, 'Have this with the compliments of the committee. The pictures are distributed over two rooms; start in this one and follow through chronologically.'

The first room housed examples of Tate's work from his student days to 1970, the year when he suffered his first stroke. The great majority of the forty-odd pictures were landscapes: river scenes, woodland glades, farmsteads, châteaux on the Loire, peasant villages in Greece, olive groves and beached fishing boats.

Wycliffe was not very knowledgeable about paintings or painters but the Impressionists had seemed to give him a glimpse of a world before the Kaiser's war, of life

164

on the other side of the Great Divide. Tate had certainly painted in the style of the Impressionists, but after his first tour of the room Wycliffe felt disappointed, without knowing why. Perhaps it was too large a dose of the same medicine, but many of the pictures struck him as sentimental and indulgently nostalgic.

Could it be that the Impressionists painted their world as they saw it while here was an imitator? He thought that over. At least it was something moderately sensible to say to Burger.

Before he could go on to the second room Burger came bowling swiftly over the polished floor. 'Well?'

The old man listened to his diagnosis with interest and some amusement. 'Poor old Gifford! "Sentimental and self-indulgent". Well, there are critics who would agree with you, but now have a look at the other room and see if you revise your opinion.'

There were fewer pictures in the second room: less than twenty, and Wycliffe was immediately struck by their greater vigour; the colours were stronger, on the whole, and there was greater contrast. Nature was still the dominant theme but these were pictures of the contemporary world seen through the eyes and with the mind of a man who happened to employ Impressionist techniques.

Burger gave him little time to consider his judgement before joining him again, and he felt like a schoolboy being tested on his homework.

Burger said: 'These strike you as very different?'

Wycliffe ventured: 'They seem to represent a change of attitude.'

'Yes. With very little change in technique; remarkable, isn't it?' Burger's grey eyes were watching him. 'Angela Bice, the art critic who did the blurb for the catalogue, puts it down to his stroke which she regards as a "seminal event in his life". Art critics talk like that. She sees it as "the first real set-back in his career and therefore a challenge".' Burger smiled. 'It's true that Gifford enjoyed a pretty smooth run until then; his father left him well off, he had good health, his pictures sold, and women found him attractive. What more could a man want?

'Then, almost from one moment to the next, he's paralysed down one side . . . He took it badly at first, and no wonder!'

'But he rose to the challenge,' Wycliffe said, in order to say something.

'And rather magnificently, don't you think?'

Burger was up to mischief, that much was clear, but Wycliffe could not fathom what particular mischief.

He went on: 'I've spent a lot of time here while they've been setting this up.' A broad gesture, taking in the whole display. 'Although I was on intimate terms with Gifford for fifty years I've never before seen the whole range of his work gathered together in one place. It's been an interesting and instructive experience to see his pictures chronologically arranged.' He looked up at Wycliffe with another of his enigmatic little smiles. 'Death and rebirth at sixty-three! I hadn't realised until now what a dramatic metamorphosis it had been. Perhaps that was why Edwin was so anxious that I should buy new spectacles.'

Wycliffe, floundering, said: 'I gather from Cathy Carne that Edwin was very much looking forward to this exhibition.'

'I'm not surprised. I don't doubt that he expected to enjoy himself enormously, though what the outcome would have been – what the outcome will be – I don't know. Incidentally, in case it interests you, both my

Tates belong to his later period. The first was painted soon after his stroke, and he very generously presented it to me, perhaps a sort of celebration of his invigorated talent.'

Wycliffe was well aware that the old man, in his oblique fashion, had been telling him something of importance; he realised, too, that direct questions would get him nowhere. He needed time to think, time at least to work out the right approach.

Almost in self-defence, he moved on to firmer, factual ground. 'There is one question I want to ask you – not about pictures: did you, or Garland, or Tate, to your knowledge, ever own a hand gun?'

A deep frown. Burger was conscious of the change of roles, he was being interrogated. He answered after a moment's thought: 'I never did, and I'm reasonably sure that Edwin didn't either.'

'And Tate?'

Burger hesitated again. 'Well, I do know that he bought a gun during our last Mediterranean trip. Our idea was to sail round Sardinia, and with all the tales of bandits one heard he thought it as well that we should have some means of defending ourselves.'

'When was that?'

'In '69, the year before he had his stroke.'

'You went in your own boat?'

'Good heavens, no! We crossed from Genoa on the regular service and hired a boat with a Sard crew-man in Asinara. It was in Genoa that Gifford bought his pistol – an automatic of some sort, I think.'

CHAPTER TEN

It was five o'clock, the wind had dropped, the sun was hot and the street was almost empty. The holiday-makers were getting what the brochures had promised. It was Sunday afternoon and Wycliffe felt the need to walk in the sunshine, to ventilate his lungs and his mind. Through the street, he went past the Thomas Garland house and the docks and across the narrow neck of land still marked by Cromwell's earthworks, thrown up when his men besieged the castle. Wycliffe arrived at the sea-front and the beaches. His mind was occupied by seemingly casual recollections of things people had said, things he had been told. He could always more easily recall the spoken than the written word. Phrases and sentences seemed to drift to the surface of his mind and he played with them, linking, rearranging, and eventually discarding those which seemed not to fit. This was the mind game which he sometimes called musical chairs.

He walked along the sea-front and stopped to lean on the rail where he could see the beach. The Falmouth beaches are small and rather steep compared with the great stretches of flat sand on the northern coast. Swimming is good, surfing almost non-existent. There is a family picnic atmosphere quite unlike the narcissistic-maximum-exposure sun cult of the other coast. Pleasantly nostalgic.

Wycliffe had started by thinking about the fringe provisions of Edwin's will:

£1,000 to Alan Tate – 'the son of my friend Gifford Tate together with my tube of Winsor blue.'

£1,000 to Martin Burger '. . . for that new pair of spectacles which I hope may improve his judgement and help him to see the obvious.'

'Winsor blue is the trade name for an artists' colour . . . Gifford Tate started to use it as soon as it came out, he said it brought him luck. Uncle used to tease him about it . . .'

'. . . the old man wrote Cathy Carne a letter which I was charged to pass over unopened.'

'I hadn't realised until now what a dramatic metamorphosis it had been. Perhaps that was why Edwin was so anxious that I should buy new spectacles.'

'Uncle was really looking forward to that exhibition.'

'I don't doubt that he expected to enjoy himself enormously though what the outcome would have been – what the outcome will be – I don't know.'

Wycliffe sighed and continued his walk along the seafront. Well, it might have been obvious but Burger himself had only recently tumbled to it and the old fox hadn't come out in the open even now. Only hints, with the implied invitation to make what he could of them.

He completed the circuit, arrived back in the main street, and made for the Incident Room. DC Curnow, the blond giant, was duty officer. Curnow had two obsessions, rugby and self-education. Rumour had it that he was working his way through the Encyclopaedia Britannica and that he had reached E.

Wycliffe put through a call to the Burger house and spoke to Mrs Burger: 'I wonder if it is possible to speak to your husband?'

Burger must have been close by for almost at once his suave, cultured voice came over the line. 'Mr Wycliffe?'

Wycliffe thanked him for the preview. 'I think that I have now understood your remarks but I shall be grateful if you will enlarge on them a little. If I might come and see you at some convenient time . . . ?'

Burger was polite, dry and evasive. 'If you are seeking an opinion on a series of pictures you should call in an expert. I am by no means an authority and my opinion would carry no weight.'

'I was hoping for confirmation of what I understood you to have said.'

A pause. 'I think you have understood me quite correctly but I am afraid that you must look elsewhere for verification.'

There was nothing for it but to thank the old man and leave it there. He had scarcely expected an open acknowledgement, let alone co-operation. All the same it was a set-back. Experts would take for ever and it is their function to disagree. In the meantime . . .

Cathy Carne was certainly not an expert but he suspected her of having knowledge of more practical value. He turned to Curnow: 'I shall be back in an hour if not before.'

He walked along the wharf to the printing works. Church bells were ringing for Evensong. Although sunset was still hours away an evening calm was settling over the harbour and town. On the south coast there is a serenity and a solemnity about fine summer evenings which can be vaguely depressing. It reminded Wycliffe of Heber's hymn about Saints casting down their golden crowns around a glassy sea.

Cathy Carne had lost something of that air of smooth competence which had impressed him at their first meeting. She looked tired and careworn and she was by no means pleased to see him though she did her best to conceal it. The flat, too, was showing signs of unusual neglect: the bedroom door stood open revealing an unmade bed. In the living-room the pages of a Sunday newspaper were scattered over the floor and there were crumbs on the carpet. On a low table there was a tray with a mug of tea and two or three roughly cut sandwiches on a plate.

'I was having tea. Can I offer you something?'

Wycliffe refused.

'You won't mind if I carry on?' She did it to keep in countenance.

'I suppose you have heard that Mark Garland is missing?'

'*Missing?*'

'It was on the local news at lunchtime; in any case, I thought Dr Tate might have told you.'

'I didn't listen to local radio at lunchtime and although Dr Tate is a friend we don't live in each other's pockets.' Snappish.

'So he hasn't told you either that Mark was having a homosexual affair with Francis?'

She paused with one of the sandwiches half-way to her lips. 'Mark and Francis? I can't believe it!'

'They met regularly at Brand's place. Last Tuesday they had a jealous quarrel; that was how Francis came by his bruised face.'

She gave up any pretence of continuing with her tea; she put the sandwich back on her plate, pulled down the hem of her skirt, and seemed to brace herself.

Wycliffe could not make up his mind. Was she really hearing all this for the first time?

The dark blue eyes studied him with disturbing intensity. 'You think Mark killed him; is that it?'

'That is one possibility, but there is another: that Mark too has been murdered.'

Her response was instant. 'I can't believe that! Why should anyone want to kill Mark?'

'Perhaps for the same reason that Francis was murdered – because he knew something which threatened the killer. I've warned you already that you may be running that kind of risk yourself.'

She turned on him angrily. 'And I have told you that I don't know what you are talking about!'

In almost convulsive movements she crossed her legs and clasped her hands about her knees. 'You don't give up, do you? As it happens I've made up my mind to tell you what was in Uncle's letter because I realise that I shall have no peace until I do.'

'Go on.'

'I didn't want to – not because it effects me but because it concerns Beryl and Francis.'

Wycliffe wondered at this sudden consideration for her cousins.

'Uncle thought that I might have misgivings about accepting a substantial share of his property and depriving them of what they might look upon as theirs by right.'

'So?'

'He told me in his letter that neither Beryl nor Francis were his children, both were illegitimate; their true father was a man called Jose, an estate agent.' She reached for her cigarettes. 'Does that satisfy you?'

'No. It's a good try but that affair between Edwin's wife and the estate agent has entered into folklore; Edwin must have known that it was common knowledge and he also knew you too well to suppose that you would be unduly troubled about your cousins' feelings anyway.'

She lit her cigarette with a concentrated effort at composure. 'Be as unpleasant as you like but I've told you what there is to tell.'

'All right, leave it for the moment. Let's talk about paintings: you won't have had a chance to see the Tate exhibition yet but—'

'I have seen it; Papa Burger invited me to a sneak preview this morning.'

'Then you must have noticed the differences between the paintings in the two rooms. I'm not knowledgeable about painting but one could hardly miss them.'

She made a gesture of impatience. 'Of course there are differences. What do you expect when a man resumes painting after a severe stroke? He's not going to take up his brush just where he left off.'

Wycliffe leaned forward in his chair. 'Let's stop playing games. You've known since last Thursday, when you read your uncle's letter, that Tate never painted a single picture after his stroke. All the subsequent work attributed to him was painted by your uncle.'

She was silent for a moment or two, watching him through the haze of her cigarette smoke, then she made up her mind. When she spoke she seemed to be mentally ticking off her points, and her manner was contemptuous. 'Gifford Tate's pictures have been studied and written about by experts, there are several of his earlier and later works in national collections, here and abroad; all his pictures are handled by a prestigious London gallery and many have been bought by notable connoisseurs. Don't you think it surprising that no one has noticed a fraud?'

Wycliffe sounded bored. 'I've nothing to say about art experts and you have no need of their opinions as far as Tate's work is concerned; you know the facts, and you have the word of the man who painted about a third of the pictures in that exhibition. I doubt whether his letter to you came as a complete surprise but that doesn't matter.'

'You are saying that Tate allowed my uncle to use his name and imitate his work over a period of several years – why?'

'Well, there was a very substantial income from the pictures, but I hardly think that carried a great deal of weight. From what you and others have told me about your uncle and Gifford Tate, my guess would be that it all started as a joke – a bit of fun, possibly to cheer up Tate. The first forgery – if we are to call it that – was presented to Papa Burger as a test, and the fact that it was accepted by him as the work of a re-invigorated Tate was irresistible to the jokers. If Burger was taken in it was altogether too tempting to try it on the art world at large. It seems they lapped it up, and still do. In the words of the catalogue poor old Tate's stroke was "a seminal event" in the development of his talent. Heady stuff!'

The sun had come round to shine through the westward facing window and the golden light seemed to emphasise the dust on the furniture and the fluff on the carpet in a room that was usually immaculate.

Cathy Carne sat back in her chair as though dissociating herself from all that had been said. 'If that's what you want to believe then I can't stop you but I don't know where you are going to find the evidence or why you should want it.'

Wycliffe said: 'I don't think evidence will be difficult to come by and I shall search for it because this fraud, and his knowledge of it, was responsible for Francis's death.'

She was engaged in stubbing out her cigarette and he could not judge her reaction.

'The original hoax, dreamed up by Edwin and Tate,

was so successful that they found themselves riding a tiger – not, I suspect, that they were all that anxious to get off. The whole thing appealed to their rather malicious sense of humour and it was also very profitable.'

Cathy Carne maintained a slightly amused, contemptuous attitude. 'So why was Edwin so anxious to tell me about it when he died?'

'The answer could be that a hoax loses its point if nobody realises that it is one, but I think there was more to it than that. Edwin left it until his death to confide in you, but he had told Francis a year before.'

She could no longer sit still; she got up and walked over to the window. 'As I've already told you, Francis was the very last person he would confide in about anything.'

Wycliffe went on as though she had not spoken. 'Your uncle had a low opinion of most of the people around him and he seemed to take pleasure in the prospect of frustrating them. Think of his will in which he left the residue of his estate jointly to Beryl and Francis.'

Without turning round she said: 'I agree with you there, but—'

'The way he went about exposing the picture hoax was another example. Francis was briefed first. For a year he had the satisfaction of watching Francis, primed, ready to burst, but unable to speak without risking his expectations under the will. But if, for any reason, Francis failed to speak when Edwin was dead, you had your letter and Papa Burger and Alan Tate, their enigmatic bequests. Who would do what? Another stir of the pudding. But, of course, he wouldn't be there to see.

'As his health deteriorated one has the impression

that he became more determined to get as much entertainment as possible out of the situation, to sail nearer the wind, and so we have this exhibition which he didn't live to see. Imagine him if he had, watching the reactions as this severely chronological arrangement of pictures made its impact in moving round the country. It would be seen and reviewed by the Mandarins of the art establishment. Surely somebody would have the insight – and the guts – to blow the whistle? No wonder he was looking forward to it!'

She turned away from the window with a sigh. 'I'm not going to argue with you.'

Wycliffe got up from his chair. 'No, but just think of your position: by your refusal to talk you run a serious risk of being regarded as an accessory and, if Mark Garland was murdered, you will have contributed to his death.'

'And how would Mark Garland have come by this great secret?' She was scathing.

'Pillow talk? I believe lovers are notoriously indiscreet in their confidences. What was it that Mark was so anxious to explain to Beryl? Don't you think that when he failed he might reasonably have tried elsewhere?'

She was very pale but she said nothing. She saw him to the door and stood at the top of the steps as he went down. When she closed the door did she go straight to the telephone? Tonight he was not quite so sure. He was taking a risk, but he had to get the case moving somehow or risk worse to come.

DC Curnow handed him a polythene envelope containing a sheet of mauve writing paper. 'Pushed through the letter-box earlier this evening, sir. Just folded across, no envelope; anonymous, of course.'

Written in a round, schoolgirlish hand, the message

read: 'Thelma George says she heard a shot when she passed the Tates house Saturday evening. She works in Paynes coffee shop.'

Explicit, and more literate than most, but every major case draws the fire of practical jokers and nutters. All the same . . .

Curnow went on: 'I contacted DS Lane, sir, and she traced the girl George through the owner of the coffee shop. She's gone to talk to her. She shouldn't be long.'

She wasn't. In ten minutes Lucy Lane arrived back with the girl: a fair, skinny seventeen-year old, packaged in the inevitable jeans and T-shirt. She was nervous and resentful. 'You think you got friends and this is what they do to you.' She examined the anonymous note with distaste. 'That's Sharon James, I'd know her writing anywhere. I never wanted to get mixed up with the police.'

Wycliffe was gentle. 'But you *were* outside the Tates' house sometime on Saturday evening?'

The girl looked at Lucy Lane. 'I told her.'

'At about what time were you there?'

'About half-past eight; I was on my way to a friend's place.'

'And you heard a shot?'

'I never said it was a shot; I said I thought it sounded like a shot but I don't really know what a shot sounds like, do I? It was a sort of crack, not very loud. Anyway, who'd be firing off a gun in a place like that? I didn't think any more about it.'

'But you must have mentioned it to someone.'

'Well, yes. I was out with the usual crowd this afternoon and one of the girls whose mother works at the Tates said the police had been there about that man Garland who's missing and I just said what I heard – just for the sake of something to say.'

'I'm glad you did. Now I would like you to go with Miss Lane and let her write down an account of what happened on Saturday evening for you to sign.'

'Can I go then?'

'Of course! Miss Lane will take you home.'

Lucy Lane shepherded her into the little interview room.

A shot at 8.30 on Saturday evening at the Tates' place! It was almost unbelievable but the girl, a reluctant witness – often the best, had heard something, and the time was significant. At any rate he couldn't ignore it. He contacted sub-division and arranged for the Tate house to be kept under surveillance until further notice. No need for concealmeant. It would do the doctor no harm to find a police car outside his gates.

PC Dart in his Panda Car had taken up his position outside the gates of Tregarthen at 22.00 and it was now 02.15; nearly four hours of his shift to go. He was unaccustomed to the deadly monotony of surveillance. This was the third time he had been out of his car, walking up and down to stretch his legs and keep awake. A quiet, warm, moonlit night, no one about. The great pines in the garden of Tregarthen rose out of the shadows and towered against the sky. A motor cycle engine, muted by distance, roared briefly then faded. The whole town seemed asleep. He was standing by the drive gates when he heard a scream, followed by another, abruptly cut short. He could see twinkling lights from the direction of the house which had not been there before.

On his personal radio he called his station and reported, then he entered the grounds through the wicket gate and sprinted up the drive. There were lights in the house, upstairs and down. He reached the front door, put his finger on the bell, and kept it there. Three years in the force had not cured him of butterflies in the stomach when faced with a possible emergency. Apart from anything else he dreaded making a fool of himself.

He could hear a man's voice, measured, reassuring. A light went on in the hall and the door was opened by Dr Tate himself; he was fully dressed. Mrs Tate, in her nightdress with a dressing gown over her shoulders, was standing behind him. She looked desperately pale, but more or less composed. Tate said: 'I know you, don't I? PC Dart, isn't it?'

'Yes, sir; I heard screams.'

'Yes, I'm afraid you must have done. Mrs Tate had a distressing nightmare and, as you can see, she is still very upset. I'm going to get her a hot drink then, back to bed . . . Good night, and thank you for coming to our rescue.'

'Good night, sir . . . Madam.'

In other parts of the town PC Dart would have had no hesitation in logging a 'domestic' – a family row.

CHAPTER ELEVEN

Wycliffe, after an early breakfast, was at the Incident Room by eight o'clock but Kersey was ahead of him.

'I hear the Tates had a disturbed night, sir. Marcella is supposed to have had a nightmare.'

Wycliffe glanced through the report which had come through from the local station.

Kersey said: 'Do you believe it?'

'I'm reaching a point where I'm prepared to believe anything. You've heard about the girl who thinks she heard a shot?'

'Yes. Seems a bit unlikely, don't you think? I can't see Tate using a gun in his own house; too risky. It's not all that isolated and he's not stupid.'

'Nobody noticed Marcella's screams last night or, if they did, they didn't do anything about it. In any case people instinctively explain away something as unlikely as the sound of a shot, especially in that sort of neighbourhood. Anyway it's given us a lever with Tate; he's got a Panda car sitting outside his gate. Let him try living with that for a bit.'

Kersey selected a bent cigarette from a crushed pack and straightened it with loving care. He said: 'You think the solution lies in that direction?'

'Things seem to point that way. Any one of several people might have killed Francis, but, if Mark Garland was murdered, what we know so far suggests that he died on Saturday evening in the Tate house.'

'Because somebody saw him go in and nobody saw him come out?'

'There is also the girl's story of a possible shot at the critical time – 8.30 – and she sounded like a credible witness. But look at the alternative, that Mark Garland was the culprit, not another victim. If he intended to do a bunk would he put on his best suit, leave his car in the garage, and pay a call on his doctor without even a weekend bag?'

'Isn't it possible that he committed suicide?'

'You think that would make the suit and the doctor more plausible?'

Kersey's face, mobile as a clown's, expressed grudging acceptance. 'I must admit, put like that, it sounds better than I'd thought, but I would have expected something more subtle from the doctor. And what about motive?'

Wycliffe retailed the picture saga and Kersey listened with close attention but at the end he was still dubious. 'You are suggesting that Tate killed twice – for what? To cover up the fact that his father and Edwin Garland had bamboozled the art world for years. Is that it, sir?'

Wycliffe shook his head. 'That's not exactly what I had in mind. Anyway, I'm going to tackle Tate this morning and I want you to lay on a search of his premises this afternoon – I'll fix it with Tate without a warrant if possible. If Mark Garland was murdered, Tate's problem was or is to get rid of the body where no one will find it.'

'Would it matter if it was found?'

'I think so. Unless Tate faked a convincing suicide, Garland would lose his value as a scapegoat and our investigation would continue; in fact, it would be reinforced.'

Kersey said: 'It's not easy to hide a body unless you

can drop it overboard in deep water with a hefty sinker.'

'That's the point; and it's unlikely that Tate managed that or anything like it on Saturday night. It would be asking for trouble to risk trying by day, and we've had his place under surveillance since yesterday evening.'

Kersey exhaled a cloud of grey smoke and coughed. 'You think the body may still be on the premises?'

'If there is a body – I think it's possible.'

'So you want a search team for this afternoon. You think Tate will consent?'

'It will be interesting to find out. If not, we get a warrant.'

Another beautiful day, still with that morning freshness but with the promise of heat: Wycliffe upheld the dignity of the Force in a light-weight grey suit, with collar and tie, and knew that he would regret it later. A trickle of people made their way to the beaches, lobster-coloured parents and trailing children. He drove up to the terraces and parked near a Panda car outside the Tates'.

'PC Gregory, sir. PC Dart was relieved at six.'

'Anything happening?'

'Nothing much, sir. At 07.30 the woman who works here arrived. At 08.00 Dr Tate came out and asked me what I was doing here. I told him I was on duty and he went in again. At 08.40 a young chap in overalls drove up in a junior Volvo. He opened the big gate and was about to drive in. I asked him what was going on and he said he was from Barton's Garage. He'd come to collect Dr Tate's car for repair and he was going to leave the other as a temporary replacement. A few minutes later he came out driving the doctor's big Volvo and I saw that the off-side bumper was sagging a bit, the

182

headlamp was smashed and the bodywork damaged.'

'I know, I saw it earlier.'

'Since then, nothing except that the receptionist turned up for work at 08.50.'

Wycliffe walked up the drive to the front door and rang the bell. It was answered by a thin, grey-haired woman wearing an overall. He said: 'Chief Superintendent Wycliffe.'

She looked at him with unconcealed antagonism. 'I know who you are. I must say, you choose your time. The doctor has his surgery and there's a waiting-room full of patients. It's none of my business but I should think the police had something better to do than come pestering people like the doctor.'

Obviously a disciple.

'Who are you?'

'Me? I'm Mrs Irons. I come in daily to help out – except Sundays that is.'

Wycliffe said: 'Will you ask Mrs Tate if she will see me?'

She gave him a dubious look, unsure how safe it was to trifle with a chief superintendent. 'She's not well; she shouldn't be worried.'

'Ask her.'

He waited in the black-and-white tiled hall, listening to the grandfather clock as it grudgingly doled out the seconds. A couple of minutes went by before Mrs Irons came back.

'All right. She'll see you in her room. You'd better come with me.'

Marcella's room was between the drawing-room and the dining-room and it had a french window opening to the garden at the side of the house. Marcella, wearing a shabby, green housecoat, was sitting at a knee-hole desk with an exercise book open in front of her. Her little dog was alseep in a basket at her feet. She got up to greet him.

Wycliffe said: 'I'm sorry to intrude; I gather you had a disturbed night.'

A self-conscious laugh. 'I had a nightmare. Absurd really! I dreamt that I was being suffocated and I was terrified. I haven't had anything like it since I was a young girl and I feel really silly.'

Her voice was unnaturally loud and her manner was tense – brittle.

'Do sit down.' She pointed to a chair and sat down herself.

'It must have given Dr Tate a fright.'

'Yes, it did. Luckily he hadn't gone to bed; he was working in his surgery. Paper work; you wouldn't believe! He really needs more help. At least one night a week he's up until the small hours.'

He was shocked by the change in her appearance. In her shapeless and worn housecoat which hung about her in folds, with her haggard features and untended hair, she looked like a severely harassed housewife cultivating an addiction to Valium. But she was more ready to talk than she had been during his last visit; perhaps too ready.

'Will you tell me what happened on Saturday evening?'

She frowned, obviously simulating an effort of memory. 'Saturday evening was when Mark Garland came. I was out, taking Ricky for a walk. I went out soon after eight; I prefer it when there are not too many people about, don't you?'

'Where did you go?'

'Oh, the usual – across the sea-front. It was a lovely evening and we sat, Ricky and I, in one of the shelters for a while.'

'When did you get back?'

'After nine.'

'Was Mark Garland here then?'

'Oh, no; he'd gone. Alan told me what he'd come about but I've forgotten.'

She was well briefed.

'Did you meet anyone you knew while you were out?'

'I don't think so. I talked to a lady in the shelter but she was a visitor, staying in one of the sea-front hotels I think.'

The room was sparsely furnished: the desk, book-shelves, and two or three unmatched chairs. A couple of pictures and a few photographs impressed some individuality on the room which was otherwise tasteless and institutional. But Marcella's pictures were Tates: head and shoulders portraits; one of her, younger and plumper; the other, obviously a self-portrait, of a gentleman with a spade beard and an elaborately cultivated moustache. Looking at the man it was easy to see where Alan Tate had got his large, doggy-brown eyes.

She saw his interest. 'Gifford did them especially for me; he didn't usually do portraits and I wouldn't part with them whatever happened!'

'Of course not.'

She was staring up at the portrait of her husband with a reflective air. She said: 'I know people don't believe it but I loved Gifford, really loved him, and we only had two years together before his stroke.'

'That was very sad.'

She looked quickly at him and away again, bird like. It was odd; her naivety seemed blended with a shrewd concern about the impression she made.

'And yet his stroke made no real difference. In a way

185

it was better for me because he needed me and I had him more to myself . . . You see, he'd done everything for me, everything!' She spoke haltingly and in a low voice that was almost reverential.

'I mean, I was brought up by my mother in a council flat on social security. I never knew my father. I was very lucky to go to university but it was only like a continuation of school – I couldn't mix much because I never had any spending money.' Another fleeting glance to see the effect of her words.

'It was only after I met Gifford that I realised what real life could be like.' She picked up the exercise book from her desk. 'I told you I was writing his biography, didn't I? This is one of his diaries. There's a bit in here about the first time we met; he took the trouble to mention it in his diary. I'll read it to you.' She found the page and read a passage which she obviously knew by heart: '"After the lecture a sweetly plain little mouse with flaxen hair came up to me and asked questions in the most earnest fashion possible. She said her name was Marcella! What pretentious names parents give their children nowadays!"' She blushed shyly and closed the book. 'He got to like my name later.

'I'm going to call the biography "Renewal" because I remember him saying once: "Who could possibly want eternal life? I should be bored to distraction! Eternal renewal – well, that's a different matter. I think I might settle for that." And in a way he experienced a renewal, didn't he?' Once more she looked Wycliffe in the eyes.

'You've no idea what it all means to me!' She was on the verge of tears. 'Almost everything in this house is as it was when he was alive; the studio and his bedroom are exactly as they were . . . Sometimes in the evenings, when I am in the house alone, I can believe that *nothing* has changed. I feel that he is *here*, that I have really found a way—'

There was a knock at the door, it was opened, and Tate's receptionist came in, blonde, white coated, and peremptory: 'Excuse me. The doctor will see you now, Mr Wycliffe.'

Wycliffe said: 'I'll be along in a few minutes.'

Marcella immediately became agitated. 'No! No! You must go now. You must! You Must!' In her excitement she stood up and almost shooed him from the room.

In the corridor Wycliffe said: 'Has the doctor finished with his patients early?'

'No, he's seeing you between patients and I hope you won't keep him long; he's very busy and grossly overworked.'

Another disciple.

Tate was sitting at his desk with a selection of patients' records in front of him. He was distant but civil. He indicated a chair with a gesture.

'I suppose your visit concerns Mrs Tate's distressing experience last night though why that should interest the police I don't know.'

It was clear that he was under stress; his movements were restrained and precise, his words as carefully chosen as ever, but he looked very tired and even his spectacles failed to hide a darkening about the eyes.

Wycliffe said: 'I am here about Mark Garland's disappearance. I don't think you need me to explain your position, Doctor, but I have an obligation to do so. Mark Garland was seen arriving here, as you yourself said he did, at about eight o'clock on Saturday evening. Despite widespread enquiries we have been unable to find anyone who has seen him since. In the circumstances it is natural that we should begin our enquiry into his disappearance where he was last seen.'

Tate was looking at him with attention but with no hint of concern. 'So what do you propose to do?'

An observer might have thought that they were discussing some academic problem of no great moment to either of them.

'There is another fact to be taken into account: a passer-by, at about eight-thirty on Saturday evening, says she heard a sound like a shot which seemed to come from this house.'

'A shot?' Incredulous.

'Yes, and that information taken with the fact that on present evidence Garland was last seen in this house, makes a search of your premises inevitable. If I apply to the magistrate for a warrant I have no doubt that it would be granted but I would much prefer to conduct a search with your consent.'

Tate smiled. 'I don't doubt it. If I agree, the police have nothing whatever to lose; if I do not agree and you are successful in obtaining a warrant but find nothing incriminatory, the police will look foolish and, with other things taken into account, it might appear that I am being unduly harassed.'

'The decision is yours.'

Tate studied his finger-nails for a moment or two, then he said: 'I am inclined to agree to your search. You are pestering me with your visits, you have a police vehicle apparently on permanent station outside my gate, and you are encouraging my neighbours to spy on me. If a search of my house will put a stop to these instrusions it might be an acceptable price to pay.'

'The search would have to be thorough and unhampered.'

'But I have nothing to hide.'

'You may wish to consult your lawyer.'

'I know my own mind, Mr Wycliffe.' Tate was gathering up certain of his patients' records into a neat pile; when he had done so, he slipped an elastic band around them. 'When will your search begin?'

'At two o'clock this afternoon. I will see that it is carried out with as little disturbance as possible. There's another matter: now that there is a suspicion of foul play in connection with Mark Garland's disappearance I have to ask you and Mrs Tate to put your accounts of what happened on Saturday evening into writing.'

'But Mrs Tate wasn't here, I've told you.'

'Then she can say so in writing. But we will leave it until this afternoon.'

Tate barely controlled his annoyance. 'I think you should tell me, Chief Superintendent, what possible reason I could have for wanting Mark Garland dead. Surely to qualify as a major suspect one has to satisfy criteria based on means, opportunity – and motive.'

It was Wycliffe's turn to consider his words. 'All I can say is that if Mark Garland was murdered it was because he knew why Francis Garland died and who had an interest in his death.'

'And that implicates me?'

Wycliffe returned his stare. 'Only you know the answer to that with certainty, Dr Tate. Just one more request: I would like to take another look around your father's studio while I am here.'

The doctor did not answer at once, his hands clenched but immediately relaxed again. 'If you wish. Miss Ward, my receptionist, will give you the key.'

Miss Ward met him in the passage. 'You will have to come through the kitchen.'

She gave him the key and let him out into the courtyard. 'Lock the door when you've finished and put the key in the kitchen.'

The sun had not yet come round to the back of the house and it was deliciously cool under the green glass roof. Presumably it was here that Gifford Tate had relaxed during his last summer, that blazing summer of '76, while his young wife sat naked in one of the cushioned chairs, reading from the page of Proust's *Remembrance of Things Past*. Refined titillation for the elderly and the impotent; a scene from a Grecian vase: Satyr with Maiden.

Wycliffe wanted to look at the studio again in the light of what he had learned from Burger. It was the place where Tate had spent most of his time after his stroke, much of it in company with Edwin Garland.

There were too many strands. Changing the metaphor, he felt like a juggler trying to keep too many balls in the air at once.

As he passed the window of the waiting-room all the chairs seemed to be occupied and he suspected that Tate had been concerned to cut short his conversation with Marcella.

He crossed the grass to the studio, climbed the steps and unlocked the door. The substantial timber building was cool in the heat and the north-facing windows excluded the glare of the sun so that the big room seemed dimly lit in contrast with outside. He had seen it all before, but now he was seeing it with new eyes: the pot-bellied iron stove, the coal bucket, the deep, leather armchairs drawn up on either side, and the chess-board between.

Gifford and Edwin. He could imagine them on a winter's afternoon in front of a glowing stove: Gifford, in the early stages of convalescence, and depressed; Edwin, trying to kindle a spark. They would be smoking, both of them against doctor's orders; Gifford, his pipe, Edwin, his homemade cigarettes. There were

190

paper spills in a pot by the stove. From the time of Gifford's stroke it seemed they had seen less of Burger and so, perhaps, they were drawn closer together.

No doubt it began with idle talk. 'Wouldn't it be a laugh if . . . ?'

And later: 'Why not try it?'

A heartening chuckle from Gifford. 'Make a present of it to Papa and see what he makes of it.'

Schoolboys planning mischief.

Wycliffe brought himself back to the here and now. In the afternoon he would have the house and grounds searched, now was his chance to take a look around the studio. Not that he would find anything; Tate had been unconcerned about leaving him alone there. Mechanically, he went through the cupboards and drawers but he made only one discovery: a cupboard full of bottles and glasses: sherry, port, whisky, vodka, gin . . . The tuck box.

There was nowhere in the studio where a body might have been hidden; he even examined the floorboards and satisfied himself that they had not been lifted since the place was built.

With a certain reluctance, he locked the door and crossed the grass to return the key. The numbers in the waiting-room seemed hardly to have changed.

He had no doubt that Mark Garland was dead, that he had been shot, and that the shooting had taken place in or around this house. The pistol could easily be disposed of or hidden, and it might remain hidden despite his intended search. The body was a different matter. Tate was a clever man but he was not a magician, yet he seemed undisturbed at the prospect of a search.

Wycliffe entered the courtyard under a Moorish arch. It was certainly a very pleasant retreat, cool in the heat and sheltered from most winds. The sun was coming round. The gentle splash of the fountain was soothing and the falling water droplets glistened in the sunlight, sometimes with rainbow effects. There was a waterlily with white flowers and beneath its heart-shaped leaves orange and red fish lurked, half-hidden.

Mrs Irons, the daily woman, was in the kitchen and he handed her the key.

'Do you want to see anybody?'

'No, thank you, I'll go out around the back.'

'Suit yourself.'

As he turned back to the courtyard it occurred to him that the paving slabs immediately around the pool had been very recently cleaned; they were free of the dark lichen which 'ages' concrete or stone paving slabs and was present on all the others. Most people encourage it. His wife, Helen, offered libations of stale yoghurt to promote its growth, others preferred the pristine rawness of the builders' yard, but only the slabs near the pool had been scrubbed.

Marcella had said: 'Alan and I sometimes sit out here on warm summer evenings.'

Saturday evening had been warm and sunny. What could be more natural than that Garland should have been taken there instead of to the surgery or the drawing-room? A shooting indoors is likely to leave traces which are difficult or impossible to remove or disguise. How much simpler . . . And the paving slabs had been scrubbed. There was an independent witness to Garland's arrival but only Tate's word for what had happened afterwards and, according to him, he had been in the house alone.

Wycliffe looked about him with new interest. His eye was caught by something glistening on the very edge of the pool nearest to him. He stooped to see what it was and found a small groove in one of the slabs. Tiny quartz crystals in the concrete, freshly exposed, were catching the light . . . Was he letting his imagination run away with him? He went back under the green glass roof to fetch one of the lounging chairs and saw Marcella watching him through the kitchen window. Let her watch.

He placed the chair fairly close to the pool and stood behind it. The head and neck of anyone sitting in the chair would come above the back of the chair and, as far as he could tell, a bullet fired from about that position might graze the edge of the pool before entering the water . . . He put the chair back where he had found it. This was work for the experts.

He walked round the house to the drive and down towards the gates. The resinous scent of the pines, distilled by the heat, filled the air. From the drive there were tantalising glimpses of the harbour and of Trefusis fields beyond. The Tates lived in a very pleasant house in a large secluded garden; they were in good health, they were still short of middle age, and yet . . . He wasn't sure what it was he was trying to express, unless it was a sense of incongruity between these people, this setting, and violent crime.

Alan Tate seemed to value a calm orderliness in the pattern of his days. When his father died and left him the house he had given up a fairly prestigious consultancy to move back home and set up as a GP in a small town. He had kept his contacts to a minimum; he had accepted his father's young wife as housekeeper and left her free to fantasise over his father, the elderly Prince Charming who, she claimed, had awakened her to life.

For eight years it had seemed to work, until that Wednesday morning, the day of the funeral, when

Francis had arrived with a picture under his arm. Had the story which Francis had to tell come as such a devastating shock that murder seemed the only way out?

Wycliffe found himself outside the Tate's gate, standing by his car, conscious of the curious gaze of PC Gregory. He was preoccupied and decided to walk, so he left his car where it was.

Walking downhill, or down steps from the terraces, it is difficult to avoid reaching the main street, so he did not plot a course and, half-way down, after a flight of steps, he arrived in a quiet cul-de-sac, a row of colour-washed little houses opposite a disused burial ground and a yard at the end with a sign on the double gate: Barton's Garage. Car-body Repair Depot. Presumably where Tate's car was under repair. A steep slope and another flight of steps and he was in the main street.

'Fox, Curnow, Dixon and Lucy Lane, that makes four; five with you. Lucy will probably have to cope with Marcella as an extra.'

Wycliffe, Kersey and Lucy Lane in planning session. Kersey was not altogether happy. 'I take it the team will be searching for a .32 automatic and/or Mark Garland's body. Do you think they stand any chance of finding either?'

'They will also be looking for evidence that a shooting did take place on the premises and that could be a better bet.'

It was very hot in the Incident Room, all the windows were open but there was not enough movement of the air to stir the papers on the tables. The sky was blue and so were the waters of the harbour; there was an all-pervading stillness. If there was any sailing it must be going on out in the bay where they might just catch the whisper of a wind.

Kersey lit a cigarette and stared out of the window. 'Tate must have got rid of the body if there is one or he would have tried to stall the search.'

Wycliffe said: 'Has anyone found a decent place for a light lunch?'

Lucy Lane volunteered: 'If you're willing to trust my judgement, sir.'

'Implicitly.'

'It's called Twining's and it's just around the corner from here.'

She took them to a place not far from the car-park where they had a seat by a window overlooking the harbour. *Ratatouille au gratin* and a bottle of hock. They were disputing whether a light lunch could be stretched to include a dessert when Wycliffe was called to the telephone. It was Potter at the Incident Room.

'I heard you say where you were going for lunch, sir. You're wanted at the Tates' house urgently. Dr Tate has been found in his surgery, shot through the head, he's dead. PC Gregory reported on the telephone from the house just before one o'clock.'

CHAPTER TWELVE

Wycliffe stood looking down at the doctor's body which had slumped on its left side between the chair and the desk, the head towards the window, resting on the carpet which was stained with blood. There was a smallish hole in the right side of his head just above and in front of the ear pinna. His right arm rested limply behind his thigh as though it had slipped into that position as he collapsed. Wycliffe could see the pistol under the desk and slightly in front of the body. The swivel chair was farther from the desk than it would have been in use, probably pushed back as the body slumped sideways.

On the face of it, suicide.

The spectacles, their thick lenses apparently undamaged, were lying at a little distance from the dead man's face, the dark brown eyes were open and staring.

'A compassionate man,' Burger had said.

The little clock on the desk, flicking the seconds away, registered 29 minutes past one. Less than three hours earlier he, Wycliffe, had been sitting in the patients' chair on the other side of the desk. The bundle of medical records about which the doctor had slipped an elastic band was still there. Wycliffe shuddered in a brief spasm of revulsion against himself and his job; for an instant he was overwhelmed by guilt. He had not caused this man's death but if he had foreseen it, as he might have done . . . Then professionalism came to his rescue: no sign of a note.

Kersey had taken over the dining-room where there was a telephone, and Wycliffe joined him there. PC Gregory was making his report; a lean, dark man in his thirties with enough experience not to be flustered.

'At 12.45 I heard what I took to be a shot though, I must admit, if it hadn't been for all that went before, I might not have thought so. I reported in on my radio then I ran up the drive to the house. I tried the door but it was secured. I rang the bell but didn't wait for an answer. I went round to the back; the waiting-room door was locked so I found my way through the courtyard to the kitchen. That door wasn't locked but it was on a chain and I couldn't get in. In the end I smashed the glass of the kitchen window and climbed in over the sink.

'I couldn't hear anything at all. I called out but there was no answer. I went through the kitchen and into the passage and found Mrs Tate standing in the doorway of the surgery. She was sort of holding herself with both hands and when she saw me she said: "He shot himself! He shot himself!" and she kept on saying it. She seemed dazed. I could see the doctor behind the desk. I made sure nothing could be done for him then I got Mrs Tate in here and I telephoned. I called the Incident Room at 12.57.'

Kersey said: 'What time was it when you actually got into the house?'

The man shook his head. 'I don't know, sir, but with one thing and another I think it must have been at least five minutes after the shot before I was actually in the house.' He looked uneasily at Wycliffe who was gazing at him heavy-eyed.

Kersey said: 'That's honest anyway. Did Mrs Tate say anything more?'

'Not a word, sir. She seemed completely dazed and she let me guide her around as though she had no will of her own.'

'Any idea where the cleaning woman was in all this?'

'She left at twelve, sir. She lives close by and she goes home from twelve till two to give her husband his lunch.'

'All right, when your relief arrives, go back and write your report.'

The front doorbell rang and Wycliffe said: 'That'll be the police surgeon. Don't forget the coroner's office.' He went to meet the police surgeon, a young, unassuming Scot, sandy haired, with freckles.

'Dr McPherson.' The two men shook hands.

'He's in his surgery.'

McPherson followed him down the passage to the surgery, glanced about him with professional interest at his colleague's furniture and fittings, then bent over the body. A very brief examination with the minimum of disturbance. 'Well, you don't need me to tell you that he's dead or how, or when. It's a sad business; he'll be missed by his patients and by some of us. He was a first rate physician and a good GP. I don't mind admitting he's helped me out more than once. Will you be wanting me for the PM?'

'I think the coroner will nominate Franks.'

A look of surprise. 'For a suicide?'

'There may be wider implications.'

'I see. Well, I won't say I haven't heard talk about police interest but I never imagined . . .'

'Will you see Mrs Tate?'

'Ah, yes, Marcella. Where is she?'

'Upstairs, a woman officer is with her. I gather she's in shock.'

'I can believe it.'

Wycliffe was making a painful effort to come to terms with what he believed to be his own failure. 'A compassionate man, a first-rate physician and a good GP.'

Sergeant Fox, the scenes-of-crime officer, arrived and there was a telephone call from Dr Franks, the pathologist. Wycliffe took the call in the dining-room.

'I've just had your message, Charles. As it happens I'm in Plymouth and my secretary phoned through. I can be with you in about 75 minutes.'

Wycliffe, always mildly irritated by the ebullient doctor, snapped: 'The man is dead, there's no point in maiming somebody else to get here.'

Franks was notorious for fast driving.

'They'll direct you from the Incident Room on the Wharf car-park.'

He could hear a woman's voice raised in the kitchen and found Mrs Irons, the cleaning woman, confronting DC Curnow. She seized on Wycliffe, wide-eyed and trembling: 'He says the doctor is dead!'

'I'm afraid that's true.'

'But how? I mean, what's happened? He was all right when I left . . .'

'We don't know exactly what has happened.' He was sorry for her; she seemed deeply distressed.

'Where is Mrs Tate?'

'She's up in her bedroom; a doctor is with her.'

'Then I'm going up.' Challenging.

'Yes, I think that would be a good idea. Just a couple of questions first: When you went to lunch where were the doctor and Mrs Tate?'

Through her tears she said: 'He was in his surgery and she was in the kitchen preparing lunch.'

'Nothing unusual happened?'

'Nothing!'

'Just one more question: Where is Miss Ward, the receptionist?'

'She goes as soon as she's cleared up after morning surgery and she doesn't come back until four.'

In the surgery Fox was photographing the body from all accessible angles, and every aspect of the room. Fox was a very efficient scenes-of-crime officer; his Punch-like nose and receding chin gave him a comical profile and his conceit alienated goodwill, but he worked smoothly, with scarcely a pause, knowing precisely what he was going to do and the order in which he would do it. When he had all his photographs he recovered the pistol with the help of a long-handled forceps which gripped the trigger guard width-wise.

'I understand you don't want the body disturbed until Dr Franks arrives, sir.'

'That's right; get the pistol off to the lab straight away: dabs, and a full ballistics report.'

Fox placed the pistol on a prepared bed of cotton-wool in a cardboard box.

Wycliffe said: 'I want swabs taken from his and her hands for the rhodizinate test. Tell her that the test is routine.'

As he left the surgey Wycliffe met Dr McPherson coming to look for him.

'How is she?'

'She'll be all right. An emotional shock takes different people in different ways; her pulse rate is a bit erratic; she keeps feeling her throat, probably an hysterical constriction, and she's a bit vague. There isn't much to worry about, physically speaking, but it would be as well not to leave her alone. Rest and soothing companionship. I wondered about sending along a nurse? Mrs What's-her-name seems a decent soul but it might be better to have a professional. Do you know of any relatives?'

'None. I think she should have a nurse. What about questioning her?'

'Give her a couple of hours. I'll look in again this evening.'

Wycliffe rejoined Kersey in the dining-room.

Kersey had had time to ruminate. 'He couldn't face the prospect of a search, I suppose.' And then, as a new thought struck him, he looked up at Wycliffe. 'You're not blaming yourself?'

Wycliffe did not answer directly. 'I don't think the search had much to do with it. I think he was prepared for that.'

'What then?'

Wycliffe was standing by a french window which opened into the courtyard. 'Come out here.'

Kersey followed him out under the green glass roof. The afternoon sun was shining directly into the paved yard; the stone urns, filled with flowering geraniums and lobelias, looked like floral flags, and two lustrous dragonflies darted over the pool, dodging the water from the fountain.

Kersey said: 'Pretty! Am I supposed to see something?'

'The paving slabs near the pool, they've been scrubbed.'

'So they have!' The two of them had been associated for so long that they had evolved a pattern of almost reflex responses to each other's moods. When Wycliffe seemed more than commonly disturbed, Kersey's reaction was to fence.

Wycliffe pointed to the tiny groove in the edge of one of the slabs. 'What caused that?'

Kersey crouched down and carefully examined the scarred slab. 'A grazing bullet?'

'You think so?'

'I'm no expert but I'd be prepared to bet.'

'So the bullet, if it is one, is probably embedded in the opposite side of the pool. From this angle it would miss the fountain. It means that Garland must have been brought here when he arrived on Saturday evening.'

'Hardly the place for a medical examination.'

'No, but Garland didn't come here about his health, he came to talk about pictures. He struck me as not very bright, a rather weak character but conscientious, hard done by, and with a strain of obstinacy which made him aggressive. My guess is that he knew about the picture hoax, Francis had confided in him, but with Francis dead, the secret was too much for him. He wanted somebody to tell him what to do, so he tried the people directly concerned – first Beryl, then, when she wouldn't see him, the Tates. A preparatory telephone call, his best suit to boost his ego, and he presents himself.'

'You don't think he was trying his hand at black-mail?'

'I don't, but the fact that he knew, was enough to finish him.'

Kersey indulged in one of his grotesque parodies: '"Let's talk in the courtyard, it's lovely out there this evening . . . Make yourself comfortable . . . Would you care for a drink? Long and cold? Coffee if you prefer . . ." Then the poor bastard gets it in the neck – literally.'

'It could have been something like that, I suppose.' Wycliffe shivered. 'I hate this place!'

Kersey went back under the glass roof and dragged forward one of the metal chairs with its loose, striped cushions. He placed the chair with care, eyeing the scarred slab. When he sat in the chair his head came well above the cushions.

'I think this is it, sir.'

'I went through the same antics this morning.'

'And he saw you?'

'She did.'

A quick, comprehending glance from Kersey. 'Ah! . . . So where do we go from here?'

'Tell Fox to leave the surgery for the present, that can wait until after Franks has been. Start him off on this and give him what helps he needs. I shall be back in . . . Anyway, you know what to do.'

Kersey looked at him with concern. 'Something wrong, sir?' Kersey was troubled.

'Yes, an unnecessary death.'

Wycliffe left Tregarthen and retraced the route he had taken that morning, down the steps and into the secluded cul-de-sac where Barton's had their car-body repair shops. The front doors of some of the little houses stood open to the sunshine.

A first rate physician and a good GP.

He walked to the end of the street and into Barton's yard which was built up on three sides with sheds of varied structure and size. Just inside the gate there was a little building labelled 'Office' and a young girl typist told him that the foreman was in the stores on the other side of the yard.

'Are you the foreman?'

Thirty-five, dark, wearing greasy overalls and sporting a Mexican moustache. 'That's right.'

Wycliffe showed his warrant card. 'Chief Superintendent Wycliffe. I believe one of your men fetched Dr Tate's car this morning to carry out repairs.'

'Is there something wrong about it?'

'I would like to see the car.'

The foreman, puzzled, and a little worried, led the way to another shed where Tate's car had been stripped of the front over-ride, the near side lamp housing and wing panel.

Wycliffe's manner was unusually curt, almost aggressive. The truth was that he was tense and angry but his anger was directed against himself. An unnecessary death.

'When did Dr Tate have his accident?'

The foreman inspected a job sheet clipped under the screen wiper. 'The 5th, a week ago today. It was nothing much, somebody backed into him on a car-park. The insurance rep inspected the damage at the doctor's place on Friday and authorised the repair. Dr Tate arranged for us to collect the car on the 12th – that's today, and we did.'

'When was that arrangement made?'

'He telephoned on Saturday, I took the message myself.' The foreman plucked up courage. 'Don't you think you should talk to Dr Tate about this?'

Wycliffe said: 'The doctor is not able to talk to me. How long were you expecting to keep the car here?'

'We budgeted on four days, allowing for spraying.'

Four days: days when the heat would be on; after that . . . But it would require nerve . . .

He walked round the car to the rear. 'Will you open the boot, please?'

The foreman joined him. 'I can't, sir, I don't have a key.'

'But surely your man must have had the keys to drive it here.'

'The ignition key only. Of course that opens the doors but it doesn't unlock the boot. I suppose the doctor thought we didn't need it – which we don't.'

Wycliffe said: 'May I use your telephone?'

'In the office.'

He had to make his call with the foreman and the typist listening.

It was Kersey who answered.

'I'm speaking from Barton's car-body repair shop in Cross Street. Has Franks arrived? . . . Good! Tell him I'll be in touch before he leaves. I want you to look in the desk for car keys, possibly a spare set; also get Franks to look in Tate's pockets . . . I'll wait while you check.'

For three, four . . . possibly five minutes the little office seemed to exist in limbo. The typist sat at her machine staring out into the sunlit yard while the foreman pretended to be occupied in turning the pages of a trade catalogue. A clock on the wall, advertising a brand of tyres, showed ten minutes to four.

Wycliffe stood by the girl's desk, still as a graven image.

A cross between a saint and a witch doctor.

Kersey came back to the phone.

'Send down what you've got . . . now, at once. I'll be in touch.'

He replaced the telephone. 'I shall be outside.' He walked out into the sunshine and stood by the gates, waiting. It was very quiet, just a murmur of traffic in the main street. One of the high days of summer, with perfect weather, one of those days which would colour the memories of thousands of people in the winter ahead and persuade them to send for next year's brochure. To him it all seemed as remote as another world.

An unnecessary death.

A police car nosed along the street and pulled up by the gates. He was handed a brown envelope. 'From Mr Kersey, sir.'

'Pull into the yard and wait.'

Two sets of keys – different, and an odd one which seemed to match one of the others. With luck . . .

The foreman, without a word, followed him back to the shed where Tate's car was. Wycliffe went to the back of the car and inserted the odd key in the lock of the boot. It fitted. He lifted the lid. The boot was large; it held a heavy-duty polythene bag and through the semi-transparent plastic he could see the form of a man crouched in the posture of an embryo in the womb.

The foreman spoke in a whisper: 'Christ Almighty!'

Back to the little office. The girl looked up at the foreman. 'What's up, Jack?'

The foreman shrugged and said nothing.

Wycliffe picked up the phone. 'Perhaps you will leave me alone in the office for a few minutes?'

The two of them went out without a word and stood in the yard, talking in low tones.

Wycliffe spoke to Kersey, then to Dr Franks; he was on the phone for nearly ten minutes. When he had finished, the girl, looking dazed, went back into her office and the foreman listlessly set about picking up bits of junk around the yard and carrying them to the scrap pile. Wycliffe had another wait in the sunshine.

Fox and Curnow arrived in the scenes-of-crime van, closely followed by Dr Franks in his Porsche. The pathologist, tubby, immaculate, and jaunty as ever, greeted Wycliffe: 'Lovely day, Charles! Too good for work. Where is he?'

Wycliffe, sombre and taciturn, led the way to the shed where Tate's car was housed.

Fox and Curnow set to work placing flood lamps in the rear of the shed where the lighting was poor. Fox, with his conspicuous nose, receding chin, and stalking

206

gait, reminded Wycliffe of some stork-like bird absorbed in the serious business of nest building. Work in the yard had come to a stop and half-a-dozen men in overalls gathered to watch but they kept their distance.

Wycliffe called over to the foreman. 'Can the car be driven?'

'No reason why not.'

When Fox had taken his photographs of the body in situ the car was driven out of its shed; the body, still in its plastic envelope, was lifted out of the boot and laid on the floor in the empty shed so that Franks could make his preliminary examination. Apart from the pathologist only Wycliffe and Fox were in the shed with the body. It was a macabre scene with the three men bending over the encapsulated corpse under the powerful lamps.

Franks said: 'Like a giant embryo in its caul.'

The heavy polythene bag, of the sort used to pack mattresses, had been carefully sealed with a broad strip of adhesive bandage. Franks cut the bag away and exposed the body so that they saw it plainly for the first time.

No doubt about indentification; it was Mark Garland. He was fully dressed: grey pinstripe suit, grey socks and shoes, pale blue shirt and matching tie. He had been shot through the base of the skull and the bullet had emerged below the bridge of the nose, shattering a relatively small area of the face. There must have been a quantity of extruded matter for some still adhered to the bag.

Franks was straightening the limbs. 'He's been dead more than 24 hours. I'd say between 36 and 48.'

'Saturday evening at 8.30?'

'I wouldn't argue with that. No more I can do here.'

The mortuary van arrived, the body was placed in a 'shell' and driven off.

Wycliffe turned to Fox: 'When you've finished here get back to Mr Kersey at the house.'

Fox said: 'We've made a start there, sir, lowering the water level of the pond.'

'Good!' Wycliffe was getting used to Fox and beginning to like him. 'Tell Mr Kersey I'll be back in under the hour.'

He left the yard and continued down the steep, narrow alley to the main street. It was quiet, very little traffic, very few people; even the locals must have made for the beaches or the boats. In the art shop Cathy Carne's assistant was perched on a stool by the till, reading. She came over to him at once.

'Miss Carne is upstairs in the flat with Miss Garland and Anna.'

'Something wrong?'

A faint smile. 'I think they're having a kind of meeting.'

Coming to terms? Beryl had said: 'I shan't let him continue to ruin my life. That's what he wanted . . . I shall come to terms in a business-like way.'

Wycliffe went through to the little hall and up the stairs. He could hear someone talking in the living-room – Beryl, being dogmatic: 'We must keep lawyers out of this until we've reached agreement.'

He tapped on the door and it was answered by Beryl.

'Oh, it's you. I've got people with me.'

'I want to talk to Miss Carne.'

Reluctantly she stood back from the door. Cathy Carne was seated on one side of the table and there was a young woman opposite her. There were coffee cups and a plate of biscuits on the table. A social occasion. It took Wycliffe a moment or two to recognise Anna. Anna had taken herself in hand; a stylish hair-cut, a well-fitting cornflower-blue dress, a coral necklace, smart shoes and a handbag. A youthful version of Cathy Carne.

Cathy took his intrusion in her stride. 'Ah, Mr Wycliffe; you want to speak to me? We were talking things over, business-wise.'

Wycliffe looked at her with a leaden stare. 'In your office if you don't mind.'

She stood up. 'I'll be back as soon as I can.'

They went down the stairs and into her office. Despite her effort to appear relaxed she looked at him with apprehension.

'Dr Tate is dead.'

She stiffened; her whole body became tense. 'Alan . . . *Dead*?' She seemed to withdraw into herself like a snail into its shell.

'Shortly before one o'clock he was found dead in his surgery; shot through the head.'

She reached for her cigarettes, her fingers fumbled with the cigarette pack, then with the lighter. Only when she had taken the first draw did she look directly at him.

'His body was slumped between the chair and the desk, the bullet entered his skull just above and slightly in front of the right ear.' He was deliberately, cruelly explicit, and for an instant there was hatred in her eyes.

'The gun was on the floor beside him.'

The little office had become a focus of tension and emotion, isolated from the world.

'He shot himself?' She stumbled over the words.

'There is something else: Mark Garland's body has been found in the boot of Dr Tate's car.'

She was watching him intently and for the first time he detected fear in her eyes. 'Why are you being so brutal to me?'

'Because you have your share in what has happened.

You have deliberately withheld information and you have lied. I feel sure that you did not destroy your uncle's letter. Unless I misjudge you, you are not the sort to destroy evidence of any sort.'

She looked at him as though she had been paid an unexpected compliment, then she opened a drawer of her desk, took out a key, unlocked the safe and handed him an envelope. 'You are quite right, I never destroy anything.'

The letter was written on the firm's paper in the old man's powerful script:

Dear Cathy,

There is something I want you to know when I am dead (if you do not know it before). Gifford Tate did not paint any pictures after his stroke; all the work attributed to him since then is mine. It started as a joke we thought up together to have fun with Papa and with the critics who are mostly imbeciles. We were more successful than we thought possible and it was too good not to keep it going. After Gifford died without letting the cat out of the bag (I thought he would have done so in his will), I set up the Ismay-Gorton annual farce in which I play the privileged role of friend and art executor of the lamented painter. You of all people will understand what a hell of a good laugh it is! (*was*, when you read this).

But I begin to want to share the joke while I'm still around to see the red faces, so I'm opening certain lines of communication (arranging leaks). Today I told Francis the whole story. I shall be interested to see how long he can keep it to himself. My guess is that greed will outweigh his yearning for self-importance and that he will hold his tongue until I

210

am gone and he is secure in his inheritance, but we shall see!

I am also trying to get a major touring exhibition of Gifford's(!) work to give the critics a better chance.

If despite all this I still die before the world has heard the joke it will be up to you to tell them about it with the help of one or two cryptic refrences in my will.

Love from Uncle Ed who now knows all – or nothing!

PS If they want more than the evidence of their eyes, tell them that Gifford always signed his work in Winsor blue and put a blob of it somewhere in the picture. I've never used it in my life. E.

Wycliffe folded the letter and put it back in its envelope. 'Nothing about destroying it there. Quite the contrary.'

She said nothing.

'Did Tate know about this letter?'

'No, there seemed no point in telling him; by the time I received it, the day after Edwin's funeral, Francis was dead.'

'And Francis had been to see the Tates on the morning of the funeral with a picture under his arm to tell them what he knew.'

'I didn't think it was up to me to make it worse for them.'

'Perhaps you were afraid.'

She made an irritable movement. 'All right! Perhaps I was, you kept telling me I had reason to be.'

She was making a great effort at self-control and her reactions were deliberate and slow. With uncharacteristic fussiness she brushed ash from the folds of her skirt as though it were an action of importance. 'You won't believe me, but Alan told me nothing of what happened. Nothing! I've only been able to guess at what's been going on. You say I've had a share in what happened but it's been a nightmare: Alan afraid to speak, and I afraid to hear.'

'And this continued when Mark Garland went missing?'

'Just the same. We exchanged purely factual information – about your visits, what you had to say, Marcella's behaviour, that sort of thing, but nothing which committed either of us to certain knowledge.'

'Yet you knew.'

She lit another cigarette; she was very pale and her hands still trembled.

Wycliffe said: 'One more question: At what time did Tate leave you on Saturday evening – the evening Mark Garland disappeared?'

'He wasn't with me—'

Wycliffe sounded weary. 'That is what he told you to say but now that he is dead, do you still need to lie?'

She shook her head. 'No! I don't need to lie; he left me shortly after nine; he said he was worried about leaving Marcella alone.'

There was a tap at the door; Cathy's assistant was standing in the entrance to the office. 'Is it all right to shut the shop, Miss Carne? It's past closing time.'

CHAPTER THIRTEEN

As Wycliffe left the shop, pleasure boats were returning from their afternoon trips and people were streaming off the pier. In the past five days three people had died; for two of them he felt no personal responsibility; he could not have anticipated their deaths. The third was a different matter. If only that morning, in the doctor's surgery, he had foreseen the possibility . . .

An unnecessary death.

He entered one of the alleys and climbed the steep slopes as though he could appease his pent-up frustration and guilt in a furious outburst of physical energy. He arrived at the gate of Tregarthen, his heart racing, breathing hard, deeply flushed.

Now there was a uniformed constable stationed outside the gate and a string of police vehicles parked in the drive. A small crowd had collected on the opposite side of the road and people were watching from the windows of the houses. If his arrival caused a ripple of interest he was totally unaware of it.

He walked up the drive and around to the back of the house. Fox and Curnow were in the courtyard, shirt-sleeves rolled up, sweating under the afternoon sun. The fountain had been turned off and they had lowered the level of the water to expose the top three courses of brickwork. Buckets, slimy with green algae, stood in a group.

Fox stooped and pointed to a scar in the lining of the

pool where the algae had been scraped away: 'There it is, sir; no doubt about that. I think we'd better lift out the whole brick to make it easier to recover the bullet.'

He came around the pool to join Wycliffe. 'As I see it, sir, Garland was sitting in one of those lounging chairs, leaning forwards – perhaps he was watching the fish; at any rate he was shot in the back of the head and he must have pitched forward on the paving. That would explain why we've found no stained cushions: all the mess was on the paving slabs.'

Wycliffe stared at the pool and said nothing and after a moment or two Fox returned to his work.

Kersey was in the dining-room juggling with sheets of paper. 'The doctor's body has gone off to the mortuary. You know what's happening down at the garage, and you've seen Fox and Curnow out there in the court-yard. Lucy Lane has gone to break the news to Thomas.'

'Marcella?'

'Oh yes, Marcella. She's still upstairs with the cleaning woman – Mrs Irons and our woman PC from the local nick. Dr McPherson's nurse arrived but Marcella sent her packing.'

Kersey lit a cigarette. 'I'm curious about the body in the boot; was it a hunch, a tip off, or what?'

'It was a hunch which seemed so unlikely that I kept quiet about it. Tate made no real protest about the search so he must have felt reasonably safe, but I couldn't see how he'd managed it. Then it occurred to me that his car had been able to leave the premises openly, also that the repair people wouldn't want access to the boot. Taken together . . .'

Wycliffe walked over to the window and stood, looking out. 'Tate foresaw the possibility of a search, and the fact that his car was due to be in the repair shop

214

for a matter of days must have seemed providential. What he did, required nerve but, if it worked, by the time he had his car back, the heat would probably be off and he would have all the time in the world.'

'Ingenious, but I can see why you kept it to yourself.'

For once exchanges between the two men were stilted and strained. They lapsed into silence and, after a moment or two, Wycliffe said: 'I'm going upstairs.'

As he reached the top of the stairs Mrs Irons, flushed and agitated, was coming down the corridor towards him. 'I'm worried about Mrs Tate; she's behaving very queer. She wouldn't take the sedative Dr McPherson left for her and she ordered his nurse out of the house.'

She looked at him with worried eyes, wondering how far she dared confide in this grim-faced policeman. 'I think she must be out of her mind, she's talking wild and saying terrible things about the doctor. I mean, I've known him since he was a schoolboy; he might seem a cold sort of man and a bit off-hand to strangers but he wouldn't hurt a fly! Nobody knows what he's done for people. And the way he's looked after her . . . I mean, it's his house; he didn't have to let her stay on, but far from turning her out, he couldn't do enough for her. It's been more like he was living in her house. And she isn't easy to live with, I can tell you! What with her nerves and going on about Mr Gifford as though he was still alive . . . Morbid, I call it!'

'Which is her room?'

'I left her in Mr Gifford's room. It's the door facing up the passage. I'm going down to make a pot of tea.'

The door was open. Gifford's bedroom was large; the furnishing, circa 1930 was massively functional. Pyjamas were laid out on the double bed and there was a padded dressing gown thrown across the foot, all in readiness for the Master. A sectional wardrobe occupied most of one wall and all the doors stood open; there were suits, overcoats, and shirts on hangers, trays of underclothes, a rack for ties and a number of small drawers presumably containing accessories. Two sections of the wardrobe were empty.

The WPC came in, anxious and solemn; she spoke in a low voice: 'Mrs Tate is next door, in her own room, sir. I think she's intending to move in here; she's taking all her clothes out of her wardrobe.'

'Has she said anything?'

'Only to Mrs Irons, not to me.'

'Go and have a break; come back in half-an-hour.'

The girl went out and almost at once Marcella came in loaded with an armful of dresses still on their hangers. She dropped them on the bed, then started shaking them out and hanging them one by one in an empty section of the wardrobe.

Wycliffe stood with his back to the window and at first she took no notice of him, apparently absorbed in her work. Then his continuing presence seemed to make her uneasy and from time to time she glanced across at him, her eyes half fearful, half defiant.

Abruptly, in the act of shaking out the creases from one of her dresses, she said: 'I'm moving back in here with Gifford. Of course I slept here before, but when he was ill he said he disturbed my rest so he made me move next door.'

Wycliffe said nothing and after a while she went on: 'You haven't been in this room before, have you?' It seemed that she was trying to divert his attention, perhaps his thoughts. 'Just like the studio, I've kept everything exactly the same here as it was before Gifford was taken ill . . . Look at all his clothes! He has always been very particular about his clothes. Alan was like him in that way . . . Always immaculate . . .'

After another silence, during which she went on putting away her dresses, Wycliffe said: 'Why have you been telling Mrs Irons that Alan killed Francis and Mark Garland?' He put the question almost casually.

Abruptly, she sat on the edge of the bed and ran her hands through her hair. 'I really don't want to talk about it any more! I should have thought I'd suffered enough.'

'I want you to tell me what really happened on Saturday night when Mark Garland came and what happened last night when you screamed.'

She looked at him, vaguely. 'Last night?'

'You said you had a nightmare.'

She pressed her hands to her head. 'Did I? I'm so muddled! Alan always told me what to say and now I don't know where I am. I don't know what I said and what I didn't; I don't know what I'm supposed to say.' As she spoke she was watching him through half closed eyes.

'It doesn't matter about what you are supposed or not supposed to say; you know what happened on Saturday night when Mark Garland was here, and you know what happened last night to make you scream.'

She nodded slowly. 'I know about last night!' She repeated with a curious emphasis: 'I know what happened then. I saw Alan with Mark Garland's body.'

'Let's start with the night before – Saturday night, when Mark Garland came. You said that you took your dog for a walk and that it was after nine when you came back. What happened then?'

She frowned and clasped her hands tightly together. 'Well, I just came in and went to bed.'

'Did you see Dr Tate?'

'Of course! He said I looked very tired and he insisted that I go straight up to bed. I did, and he brought me a hot drink in bed.'

'Did he say anything about Mark Garland?'

'Just that he'd been; I think he said something about Mark being ill or thinking he was ill; I can't remember.' She gave him one of her quick, appraising glances.

Wycliffe was silent for a while and, hesitantly, she got off the bed and resumed putting her clothes away. Somewhere in the house a clock chimed the half-hour. Six-thirty.

'Who scrubbed the courtyard?'

She turned to face him. 'Oh, Alan did. I heard him at it early yesterday morning before I was up.'

'Now tell me about last night.'

She sat on the bed again; placed her hands together between her knees and leaned forward. She moistened her lips. 'I suppose I've got to . . . It was about two o'clock in the morning; I woke up and I could see a faint light coming from the corridor. I always leave my door open a bit for Ricky. I got out of bed and I could see that the light was coming from downstairs. I went to the top of the stairs and called. Alan answered, he said: "It's all right, Marcella; go back to bed."'

She shook her head and in a low voice she went on. 'I didn't go back to bed. I went down the stairs, but before I got to the bottom the light was switched off and I couldn't see a thing. I worked my way along the wall to the switch and when the light came on I was standing . . . I was almost touching a great plastic bag . . .' She shivered. 'And in the bag there was a body . . . I could see it. Then I screamed.'

There was a long pause; she shuddered, and said, nodding her head as though she had settled some problem: 'Yes, that was how I knew for certain what he had done.'

Some truth and some lies; her own bewildering blend

218

of fact and fiction, reality and fairy tale. That would be the pattern of her response to all interrogation. Sometimes naive and sometimes cunning, she would rely on those quick bird-like glances to pick her way through the maze.

'Why would Dr Tate want to kill Francis and Mark Garland?'

She stiffened and looked at him, her eyes wide. She raised her voice. 'Why? I don't know! He didn't tell me; he never told me anything . . .'

'And you say you were out on Saturday night when Mark Garland came?'

'I keep telling you I wasn't here! Alan told you.'

The door opened very quietly and Mrs Irons came in with tea things on a tray. She put the tray down on the chest of drawers and stood, waiting. Marcella seemed not to see her.

In a low voice Wycliffe said: 'Mark Garland was shot at half-past eight on Saturday evening.'

She looked her question.

'We have evidence that Dr Tate didn't arrive home until well after nine o'clock.'

Marcella became excited: 'That is a lie! That's what Cathy Carne told you! She's been trying to . . . She will do anything! Look at the way she wormed her way in to get all she could from Edwin! For years she's been trying to get rid of me so that she could move in here with Alan!' In her frustration she beat on the bedclothes with her clenched fists.

Totally unexpected, Mrs Irons spoke in her rather harsh, masculine voice: 'It's you who is telling the lies. Ever since Mr Gifford died the doctor has looked after you and let you carry on in your own sweet way, as though he didn't exist except to dance attendance on your selfishness. Any ordinary man would have kicked you out in the first six months. Lucky for you the doctor was no ordinary man, but that's neither here nor there now; what I have to say is that I saw the doctor, coming up Quay Hill at a quarter-past nine on Saturday evening. And I'll swear to that in the witness box if I have to.'

Marcella looked across at Mrs Irons, she opened her mouth but no words came; for a long moment she seemed to be frozen, petrified; then she screamed and kept on screaming. She rolled over on the bed, kicking her feet and pummelling the clothes with her fists.

Mrs Irons looked down at her, totally dispassionate. 'Don't worry! That's nothing that a good slap wouldn't cure.'

Wycliffe wondered if Mrs Irons had really seen her doctor that evening but he had no intention of trying to find out.

Wycliffe looked and felt very tired. He was back in the dining-room with Kersey.

Kersey said: 'It didn't occur to me until we were out in the courtyard this afternoon that he was covering for her. Do you think he knew – really knew that she had shot Francis?'

'I doubt if he could have lived in the house without knowing, but he felt bound to protect her. I think that was genuine; I very much doubt if an exposure of the picture fraud would have weighed with him very heavily, certainly not to the extent of compounding a murder. What he didn't know was that it hadn't ended with the shooting on the wharf. If he'd even guessed at the possibility of another killing, then things would have been different. I don't think he would have knowingly set another life at risk.'

'He must have had misgivings about the gun.'

'She would have sworn to him that she'd thrown it in the harbour. She's a convincing liar when she puts her mind to it.'

'Then the poor bastard comes home one night to find a corpse literally on his doorstep and he's committed to something far more hazardous than keeping his mouth shut – and hers.'

Wycliffe was sitting by the window staring out into the courtyard and through the Moorish arch to the garden beyond. The low sun lit up a tiny window in the gable-end of Gifford's studio so that it seemed to blaze like a fire. He said: 'It makes my flesh creep to imagine what it must have been like for Tate in this house during that 40 hours from Saturday night to lunchtime today, with him certain now that she still had the gun. By day there was almost nothing he could do, he could only use the night when they had the house to themselves, to dispose of the body; to reason, to plead – and to search.'

'You think the case against her will stand up?'

'Yes, if it ever comes to court.'

'Unfit to plead?'

'That's what the shrinks will say.'

'And what do you think?'

Wycliffe said nothing for a time then: 'The thought of her going into the surgery, hiding the pistol, saying something quite ordinary and, as he looks up from his work . . . She needed a scapegoat and her need excluded every other consideration. That to me is wickedness. There is no other word.'

There was a long silence then Wycliffe said: 'This case has been about children, about arrested development; Gifford, Edwin and Papa Burger – they didn't grow up either. All three of them needed mothers

221

rather than wives but only Burger was lucky enough to marry one.'

And after another interval he went on: 'Three deaths to preserve this woman's fantasies. I wonder if Edwin, wherever he is, will feel now that his prank got out of hand?'

THE END

All Orion/Phoenix titles are available at your local bookshop or from the following address:

> Mail Order Department
> Littlehampton Book Services
> FREEPOST BR535
> Worthing, West Sussex, BN13 3BR
> *telephone* 01903 828503, *facsimile* 01903 828802
> *e-mail* MailOrders@lbsltd.co.uk
> (Please ensure that you include full postal address details)

Payment can be made either by credit/debit card (Visa, Mastercard, Access and Switch accepted) or by sending a £ Sterling cheque or postal order made payable to *Littlehampton Book Services*.
DO NOT SEND CASH OR CURRENCY.

Please add the following to cover postage and packing

UK and BFPO:
£1.50 for the first book, and 50p for each additional book to a maximum of £3.50

Overseas and Eire:
£2.50 for the first book plus £1.00 for the second book and 50p for each additional book ordered

---

BLOCK CAPITALS PLEASE

name of cardholder ....

address of cardholder ....

delivery address
(if different from cardholder)
....
....
....
....

postcode ....

postcode ....

☐ I enclose my remittance for £......................

☐ please debit my Mastercard/Visa/Access/Switch (delete as appropriate)

card number ☐☐☐☐☐☐☐☐☐☐☐☐☐☐☐☐

expiry date ☐☐☐☐   Switch issue no. ☐☐

signature ....

prices and availability are subject to change without notice